CAPE FEAR
MURDERS

A Carroll Davenport Mystery

CARROLL DAVENPORT MYSTERIES

Island Murders

Cape Fear Murders

CAPE FEAR MURDERS

A Carroll Davenport Mystery

by

Wanda Canada

Coastal Carolina Press
Wilmington, NC

◉ Coastal Carolina Press, Wilmington, NC 28403
www.coastalcarolinapress.org

First softcover edition 2003
Printed in United States of America

Whole copy return only

Canada, Wanda, 1941-
    Cape Fear Murders / by Wanda Canada.
       p. cm.
ISBN 1-928556-42-6
    I. Women detectives--North Carolina--Fiction. 2. Fear,
Cape (N.C.)--Fiction. 3. North Carolina--Fiction. 4.
Contractors--Fiction. 5. Witnesses--Fiction. I. Title.

PS3603.A52C37 2003
813'.54--dc21

10 9 8 7 6 5 4 3 2

Cover photograph by Bruce Patterson, Curator, Japanese
Garden, New Hanover County Extension Service Arboretum
Cover design by Maximum Design & Advertising, Inc.
Interior design by D. A. Gallagher

To: John, as always

Acknowledgments

Special thanks are owed the talented staff of Coastal Carolina Press for their endless patience, suggestions, and editing expertise.

Prologue

Near the southern boundary, a laugh drifted through foggy rain, light as air, gray as dust in the moonless midnight. When the chain fence rattled, a lone dog barked, sensing a presence three hundred feet away.

An owl in the wingnut tree shifted on a branch, ever alert to motion. Eyes were sharp enough to see movement, but the light rain confused things. He was hungry, and his ears picked up uneasy whispering near the bog, the scuff of hurrying feet across wet mulch.

Another low whisper. "Damn, I tore my new jacket on the fence. My dad is going to kill me."

"Shhh! You want somebody to hear you? We're almost there."

"It's freezing out here, Kevin, and I can't see where I'm going."

"Come on, I'll warm you up."

A satiny laugh hung briefly in the air before the dog began barking again. The pattern of the footfalls changed and picked up speed as they left the mulched area and reached the walkway.

"This way," he said. "Hurry."

Only the owl, and perhaps the dog, heard feet

cross the stones, the clunk of shoes on a wooden floor, the muffled scream.

Somewhere in a nearby house a baby was crying.

Chapter One

Liz Hunter had been dead more than eight hours before I knew about it, shot in the back of the head at close range, execution-style, on her knees in the Japanese teahouse at the Arboretum. With her was William Burris III, state senator and developer, killed in the same manner, but with his pants still down around his ankles and a surprised look on his face.

Not a very nice way to die, knowing the bullets were coming. Knowing, also, that two spouses and a total of five children would have to deal with the after-effects.

It was a Tuesday morning in late October, a regular volunteer day when I gave three hours to the Arboretum, something my eighty-six-year-old grandmother lured me into by promising a *learning experience*.

I arrived a little before eight and began pulling weeds near the perennial border, a job that lately seemed never-ending. An early hurricane had paid us a visit in mid-July, downing trees and wreaking havoc. Now we were dealing with an explosion of weeds that, I'm convinced, blow across from Africa and up the coast.

After thirty minutes, my grandmother appeared on the teahouse path, loose strands of gray hair flying. She had a Lions Club broom taller than she was flung across her right shoulder, the spring in her step belying her advancing years.

Funny, the things you remember afterward.

When you visualize tiny Southern women and energy bunnies, think of my grandmother, Eleanor Monroe, always of Wilmington. She was a Carroll, daughter of an old Wilmington family, and married into another one that settled here before the Revolutionary War. The chain would have stopped with me, Carroll Monroe Davenport, childless and widowed at thirty, were it not for her five-year-old great-granddaughter, Tully. Beyond the three of us, there's only Alexandra, my cousin Eddie's widow, all we have left of more than two hundred years of family. To balance this female mix, I live with an unpredictable Amazon parrot named Charlie who will probably outlast us all.

It was my mother's idea to give me male names. All through school I hated them, but after she drowned when I was fourteen, I never said another word. Giving offspring old inherited surnames is a way of keeping families alive, maintaining them even when the only progeny are female. It never seems to work the other way around. When was the last time you heard of a son called Mildred or Zelda?

Prospective buyers who expect men to be in

charge of construction companies are often surprised at our first meeting. A few can't get over the female thing and never call back. It's their loss. I'm good at what I do, and most of my clients, though not all, wind up as friends.

I waved and called out, "Good morning, sleepyhead. What took you so long? Did you ride in on the broom or is that your Halloween transportation?"

"You never can tell," she laughed, showing perfect teeth in a furrowed face, "but right now I'm after all those giant spiders in the teahouse. The schoolchildren love them, but I surely don't. If one of them drags me away, I'll scream. Otherwise, I'll be back to help you shortly."

I laughed. "You're braver than I am. If I never see you again, I'll know what happened."

It was her promise to scream that made me think she was joking when, less than a minute later, I heard a shriek. I smiled, certain she was kidding around, but the second scream made the hair stand up on my neck.

Chapter Two

Gran stood in the doorway of the teahouse, her chin wobbly with reaction, one thin hand pressed against her bosom. "Are they dead, Carroll? I don't think I can touch them, but shouldn't we be doing something to make sure?"

I took the broom from tight fingers and put an arm around her. Judging by the frozen stares of the two people inside, it seemed unlikely they could be anything but dead. Swallowing, I looked away from the sight of pale buttocks and matted hair.

"There's nothing we can do for them now," I said. "Come and let me find you a bench."

My grandmother had suffered a mild heart attack in the spring. I wasn't taking any chances.

She wet her lips, searching for words. "We can't just leave them."

"We won't. Just until I get some help. You've had a shock, and I don't want to go while you're standing here alone."

"Most of my friends are in caskets by now. You'd think I'd be used to bodies."

She let me help her across the steppingstones to the main path where we were met by other volunteers who had heard the screams. They ranged in age from twenty-five to eighty. Randolph Taylor was one of them, and since he worked for me, he seemed a natural choice for guard duty.

I said, "There are two people dead in the teahouse, murdered I think. Will you stand here and make sure no one goes near it, or even onto the path, until the sheriff arrives? And can you get Gran to a bench while I go phone? She'll tell you everything, but let her sit down first."

I turned and hurried through startled faces. Why, I wasn't sure. There wasn't a great rush at that point.

In the plant clinic, I used the horticulture agent's phone, closing the door before dialing my old family friend.

His secretary answered. "Sheriff Council's office."

"Janice, it's Carroll Davenport. Can you put Stan on? We have an emergency on county property."

There was a brief pause and then, "Hold on a minute."

Since an incident last spring when five innocent people almost died—one of whom was me—Janice has reacted less like a secretary protecting her boss. Afterward, she must have been dismayed to discover that when I'd called searching for Stan in a hurry, she hadn't taken me seriously. It was also possible he had given her one of his monumental storm-around-the-room reprimands. I'd been on the receiving end of those a few times myself, starting when I was eight and decided, for some forgotten reason, that my cousin Eddie's red wagon needed a hearty shove down the hill behind my house. The result was predictable. Wagon and driver were both catapulted like a rocket down forty feet of steep incline straight over the bulkhead and into the Intracoastal Waterway at high tide.

"This better be good," Stan's voice bellowed over the line. "I just walked out of a meeting with two legislators and a passel of lawyers."

"Stan, hush a minute. Senator Burris has been murdered."

I heard him inhale. "You better not be kidding me!"

"No, and that's not all. While it looks like murder, it could be a murder-suicide. There's also a woman dead with him and an indiscreet crime scene, but I don't see a gun anywhere..."

"Whoa, whoa! You're there?" He dropped his voice. "What the hell have you gotten yourself into this time?"

"Just listen. I called you rather than 911, because this one is going to need careful handling before it turns into a three-ring media circus. I'm at the Arboretum, the far back corner at the Japanese teahouse. I know it's in the city's jurisdiction, but the property belongs to New Hanover County. Can you come, Stan?"

"Are you all right? You weren't involved, were you?"

"God, no! Of course not."

"Well," he said, "I never know. I'm on my way."

"Shall I notify the Wilmington police?"

"I'll take care of it. And Carroll?"

"Yes?"

"You stay the hell out of my crime scene, you hear?"

When Stan asked what I had gotten myself into, I didn't take offense. If it hadn't been for Stan, I wouldn't be here at all.

Six months ago two of my pre-sale clients wound up dead, along with my first cousin Eddie, who had also been my business partner. Mostly I tried not to think about the other deaths in my past, some of which were decidedly worth grieving over, and others not worth the nightmares.

The small crowd had doubled by the time I got back. Gran had some color in her face, and Randolph was where I had left him, standing beside her like an aging military sentry, feet apart, hands behind his back. No one was getting anywhere near the teahouse.

He jerked his head toward the wooden structure. "Eleanor says it's Bill Burris in there with a woman. Is it true? Do you know who she is?"

"It's Liz Hunter," I said to the group as a whole.

No one exactly gasped, but you could have heard a snake slither into the pool. There were few among us who hadn't wanted to strangle her once or twice.

Liz Hunter had been thirty-nine and probably

holding, the kind of woman men love and women find mortifying, still wearing short-shorts with red slingback heels—managing to miss the trailer-park look by the skin of her sculpted nose. She was in my Master Gardener class, another learning experience Gran and Randolph had convinced me I needed. For sixteen weeks, I watched her use sexuality like a scented lure and every male member of the class, no matter the age, like a private harem in training.

Saturday workdays would never draw the same numbers again. The men came to watch Liz pull weeds, the women to watch the men and see what she would wear next. And since most of the volunteers were retirees, it added a certain amount of spice to their volunteer hours, a kind of zing that could never be matched tutoring second graders.

No, I didn't much like or admire her, but I wouldn't have wished her murdered, either.

Bill Burris I knew mostly from homebuilder association dinners, political meetings, and occasional social functions where I was careful to avoid his wandering hands. He had an office across Oleander Drive from the Arboretum, and he often dodged traffic at lunchtime to stroll the gardens with a cell phone to his ear.

There was gossip weeks ago that Liz had gone to work for Bill not long after she finished the course. I wondered at the time if she'd met him somewhere on the Arboretum's seven acres of grounds. It wasn't the first time the teahouse had been used for an after-dark rendezvous, and it wouldn't be the last.

While we waited for Stan and his deputies, I asked Randolph, "What happened to the homeless man we suspected was sleeping in the teahouse—the one with the ancient bicycle?"

"The police chased him off one night because he was spooking the women volunteers. He hasn't been back as far as I know."

"I'm not so sure," I said. "There was a bar of soap on the pool rocks last week." Better than no bath at all, I thought.

Originally, Randolph worked for my grandfather. He's a self-taught horticulturist, an African American in his mid-seventies who takes care of my three acres of grounds and lives in the guest cottage with his fifteen-year-old nephew, Davis, and a three-legged Keeshond named Max. If I had anything on the property other than vegetation, I might even call him a manager, except that he might try harder to manage me, which has been an ongoing project since he first taught me to tie my shoes. But he's funny and well read—good company in a crotchety kind of way. Much like family, if you know what I mean.

Randolph's wife, Lucille, lives with and works for Gran in downtown Wilmington on the Cape Fear River. Why the two of them lived apart was one of the great mysteries of my childhood until I heard rumors about his dalliance with another woman early in their marriage. Since I lacked the courage to ask her, I was never certain the legend of Lucille and her gun was true, but Randolph has had a gimpy leg as long as I've known him.

One of the women brought Gran a cup of tea from the plant clinic, and after that, there wasn't much talk until the police arrived, herding us back beyond the east edge of the large lily pond by stretching yellow crime scene tape from tree to tree.

An officer wrote down names and addresses of volunteers in a small red notebook. He didn't seem impressed with the ratty gardening clothes worn by the volunteers, some of whom were former doctors, lawyers, schoolteachers, and corporate heads enjoying retirement any way they chose.

"Listen up, everybody," he said. "As soon as I have your name and address, you need to go to the auditorium and wait until you've been questioned. Only then should you leave the premises. Is that clear?"

He had a lot to learn about volunteers.

A collective groan rose from the assembled cluster. Most of us were still standing around ten minutes later when Sheriff Stan Council clamped a heavy hand on my shoulder and steered me away from the others. The group parted to make room for his six-foot-eight, three-hundred-pound body.

Way back in the seventies, Stan had been a professional football player after he served in Vietnam. My father and Stan formed a friendship in the jungles, and the story goes that Stan was the reason Jack Davenport moved to Wilmington in the first place, met my mother, had me, and all the rest of the tale. Since he was around a lot when I was growing up, I seldom found him intimidating. It helped that I could beat him at poker more often than not.

He was your stereotypical Southern sheriff, but bigger and smarter than most. He was also African American, and the phrase *Boy, you're in a heap of trouble* carried a different weight when he used it. In the last two elections no one else had bothered to file for his office, a testament to the way the community felt about him.

Stan lowered his sunglasses a fraction. "I'm gonna take a quick look for myself and then will want to talk to the three of you. Why don't you round up Eleanor and Randolph and go wait in the auditorium? I'll be along in a few minutes. Anybody else go in the teahouse besides you?"

"Just Gran, and both of us were on the porch, not inside the room. Randolph blocked the path afterward so that no one got near the building."

"Good. You know more than my new-hires already. Have you heard from our friend Ben Satterwhite yet?"

"Not a word. No doubt he's found himself another woman sailing around down in the islands."

He laughed. "You think so?"

"Darned if I know what to think, Stan."

"I wouldn't worry if I were you. He'll turn up one of these days when you least expect him, maybe surprise the heck out of you."

"If the door is bolted, he might be the one in for a surprise."

He chuckled and went about his gruesome business while I collected Gran and Randolph. In the end, it took another hour and a half of waiting to repeat what little we had to tell.

Randolph grew testy after awhile, and not being blessed with an abundance of patience anyway, he wasn't shy about speaking up. "Just because we're volunteers, don't think we don't have other work to do. I can't see why we have to be questioned by every Tom, Dick, and Harriet with both the sheriff's department and the Wilmington police. Don't you people share notes? We're glad to help, Stan, but sitting around waiting and repeating ourselves is ridiculous, especially since none of us seem to know a damned thing."

As rebellious muttering erupted among the volunteers, Stan said, "I know you're all getting impatient, so let me explain. With any murder investigation, two heads are always better than one. You know that. The reason you're getting a double-jurisdiction overdose is that the Arboretum property is owned by New Hanover County, but it's also within Wilmington's boundaries. As soon as Chief Talbot finishes his budget meeting, we'll put our heads together and figure out who'll handle the case. My guess is he'll be glad to let our department have it, not only because the murders happened on county property, but because it'll be one less headache for his own department. Budgets are tight all around this year, and the city's murder rate is a lot higher than the county's."

I listened to the voices buzzing around me in the stuffy room and tried not to think about Bill Burris and Liz Hunter growing colder in the teahouse. It was hard not to wonder whether their children knew, and if not, how many more hours might pass before they learned that two of their parents were dead.

Chapter Three

I found Randolph rocking on my back porch when I got home around five o'clock. In the second chair sat a woman close to my own age, thirty or a little more, with a sailing tan and highlights in a short, stylish haircut. Even before she spoke, I had a flash of intuition. There was something about the smile wrinkles around her eyes that seemed familiar.

"Carroll, this is Mary Horne." Randolph got to his feet a second later than his guest. Neither one of them was smiling.

"What's wrong?" I said, and watched them glance at each other, as if I had interrupted a conversation before they'd decided which one would break bad news.

"I'm Ben Satterwhite's sister. You'd better come and sit down."

"What is it?" Weakness interfered with my knees. I fumbled for the rocker and sat, my eyes never leaving Mary's face, and was as sure as I had ever been about anything that I didn't want to hear what she was going to say.

For a swift second Mary looked away at the marshes, glazed yellow-gold in the autumn sun, and then back, steeling herself. "It's about Ben. His sailboat is missing."

A lone boat drifted south on the Intracoastal Waterway, its sails still unfurled in the dying breeze, moving so slowly a great blue heron cut almost across the bow and landed on the new pier.

I had to close my eyes, feeling the grayness, the tightening of my breath. Randolph's gnarled brown hand closed around mine.

It was early spring when I first saw Ben through binoculars, climbing out of a helicopter in my own backyard. I remembered with startling clarity the brown leather jacket and red tie, the sun on his hair.

When I could, I asked, "How long?"

"Two weeks. But it doesn't necessarily mean…"

I opened my eyes, taking in the grief on her face, feeling frozen in place. "I know what it means."

"Carroll," Randolph said gently, "let her finish."

"Two weeks ago, north of Eleuthra in the Bahamas, the *Blue Angel* picked up a faint distress call from another boat. Unfortunately, the *Angel* was having radio problems—receiving but not able to send—and they couldn't notify the authorities about the mayday until two days later when they reached port."

"How did *you* find out?"

"Ben was checking in every third day, mostly for my mother's peace of mind. When he missed the first date, we assumed it had slipped his mind, but by the end of the sixth day, we knew something was wrong.

Cat Island, south of Eleuthra was his last known berth, so that's where we started, eventually finding the right Bahama officials who reported they searched for three days after the original report."

"And…?" Six days. A lifetime on open water.

"Nothing. Not even another boater who heard the original call."

"How far was the *Blue Angel* from land?" Randolph said.

"A hundred miles or so."

"His distress call…" I was beginning to focus. "Was it a sudden storm, trouble with the boat, or what?"

"All the *Blue Angel* heard was part of the mayday call."

"Did he specifically hear the name of the boat?"

She shook her head. "Nothing but the word *Mary*, and it was the only distress call reported in a four-day period."

Ben's boat was *The Three Marys III*.

I said slowly, "He could have been…could be anywhere. North of Eleuthra there's nothing but open Atlantic all the way to Bermuda—six hundred miles or more."

Mary nodded. "Except he wasn't supposed to go to Bermuda. He said he didn't have time because he wanted to be home by Dad's seventieth birthday party in November. And he was going to surprise you by coming here first."

Randolph began rocking again. "Hurricane season isn't over. That's a lot of distance to cover without safe harbor. I didn't know your brother well, but from what I saw of him, he didn't seem the kind of man to go off ill-prepared for any kind of venture."

"I agree, and it might make me feel better, except for one thing."

"What?" I asked.

"If something weren't badly wrong, Ben would have been in touch. He wouldn't do this to my mother, and he wouldn't do it to you. That's really why I stopped in Wilmington on my way home from the Bahamas—to see if you had heard anything or could fill in some of the blanks."

I thought of the nights Ben had called, the sound of his deep, rich voice keeping me awake for hours afterward, missing his company, missing him. I'd had him for two whole weeks, and then he was gone. If it was for good, I might well wish I had sailed with him whatever the consequences.

"Carroll…?"

"Sorry." It was a moment before I could speak. "He left unexpectedly in March on a Bureau assignment in Idaho and didn't get back until late September. There was so little time. I mean, he was only here two weeks and I wasn't paying attention to his travel plans." I could feel the heat in my face, remembering why my attention hadn't been on his itinerary. "He said he planned to sail around the islands, maybe south to

Virgin Gorda or St. Martin, but he didn't make it that far before he turned north again. The last phone call was from New Providence, Nassau."

Mary said, "He'd planned that trip for fifteen years, just going where the wind took him, letting the sails and the blue water work their magic. After years with the Bureau, it must have been like heaven, but after a while, I think he'd had enough solitude. You were the one item he hadn't factored into those plans. Meeting you changed everything."

"Yet he went anyway," I said, my words hanging in the air, more critical than I meant. "Not without asking me to go, but we were still cleaning up from Hurricane Elizabeth and I had three houses nearing completion. If…"

"If what?" she said.

"If the opportunity ever comes my way again, I'll be packed and ready within the hour."

We sat until it grew dark and then had a simple dinner of steak, potato, and salad. While Randolph grilled, he did his best to lighten the atmosphere with amusing stories of life in and around the water.

Midway through the meal, he said, "You're not eating much, honey."

"I had a big lunch," I lied. Swallowing was becoming more and more difficult.

Everything in me felt stiff and frozen. The sliding

door facing the water was open, and a soft gust of wind suddenly swayed the chandelier crystals, casting patterns of light across the dining room table and the colorful old Heriz rug that once belonged to my grandmother.

I took a deep breath, testing a smile. "I just realized you're one of the boat Marys."

Ben had shown up again by late September in a sleek, dark green sailboat with its name in gold letters, tying up at my dock about the same time I'd decided he was never coming back, despite his promise.

She laughed. "Along with Mother Mary and Aunt Mary. There are so many Marys in the family, I don't know why we bother to use anything else. I have one myself. She's ten years old with red hair, and we're at a loss to figure out where it came from. When Ben was her age, he named his first dinghy *The Three Marys*. After that he just kept adding Roman numerals. Not very original, but we like it."

"I love to read boat names," I said. "Randolph, we should publish a book. We could write one in a single season of sitting on the dock with a notebook."

"If you could park yourself that long. I think we'd have to break both your legs and tie you to the railing, but it's worth thinking about. Maybe when I get too old to climb the hill, I'll get me a golf cart and drive it on the pier. Piece of cake."

I smiled at him, comforted by his very presence, and watched Mary study both of us, trying to figure out our relationship.

After she left around eight for a late flight back to Portland, Maine, I stood on the back patio with the lights out, feeling the warmth of the day fade, wondering if I could somehow sense whether Ben was still alive.

I waited a long time with the salty breeze in my face, watching the stars strengthen into brilliance, and had no awareness of him at all.

Chapter Four

The phone rang very early the next morning. After a brief conversation, I returned the receiver to its cradle and dressed.

The sky was just brightening. One lone star still glowed in the east as I took the Boston Whaler over to Hutaff Island and sat in wet sand while the sun crept over a flame-stitched horizon. The ocean was in a strange, sullen mood, pulling long ridges of riptides northward beyond the beach while waves shuddered and broke in different directions.

A high tide had washed the sand clean of yesterday's footprints. Except for the froth of incoming waves blowing across the sand, nothing moved—not another human soul or crab or bird. The uninhabited island could have been a thousand miles from civilization.

The red sky reminded me that we were still in hurricane season, and the thought of Satterwhite out there somewhere, lost in all that deep, limitless water, made me want to weep.

It would have been easy to give up hope that I would ever see him again.

I thought of Isabella, the reason for the early phone call, mercifully gone at last, freed from the kind of tenacious, gnawing pain that is worse than death itself. For her it had been three years coming—an eternity.

Isabella Vitelli was my mother-in-law, Daniel's mother, Sam's wife. The story is so long I hardly know how to begin, but Isabella is perhaps the easiest part of a chapter in my life that began when I was a rebellious twenty-one. It ended when Daniel was murdered, when I lost a baby and a father, suffered a nervous breakdown, and left the people I loved for two long years before returning to Wilmington.

Isabella and Sam stood by me against their own son throughout his slow descent into a drug hell—even when he was murdered in a storm of ripping bullets in our own bed with someone else's girlfriend.

I put a hand over my flat abdomen where a child would never grow now, still able to feel the knife enter as if it were days instead of years before. Through the long months in a New York hospital while I recovered from a breakdown, Isabella was a daily visitor.

Family. What a strange, heterogeneous word, conjuring up feelings of love, anger, and sorrow, molding our lives in ways we never expect. I often tried not to think about her son, but for at least three years I had hoped for a miracle for Isabella, and barring that, for the ultimate end.

Later, I would drive to Hillsborough to comfort Sam, attend Isabella's service, and be on the road home by tomorrow afternoon. What could be simpler than that? But it wouldn't be. Nothing about a Vitelli was ever simple.

Sam had tried to talk me out of coming, but I'd brushed aside his usual fears. Isabella had been like the mother I'd lost at fourteen. To her I was the link with their only son, the daughter they'd always wanted. Nothing short of a Category 5 hurricane would keep me away.

Besides, it had been more than seven years, so long that most people wouldn't remember me if I wore sunglasses and my hair up. That was what I thought at the time.

Looking back, I wonder why I was so naïve.

Davis was waiting in his great-uncle's old flat-bottomed fishing boat when I waded back to the Whaler. "Uncle Randolph said to make sure you were OK."

"Good morning. He worries too much and so do you," I said, leaning over the side of the boat and giving him a quick hug, which was easier to do when he was sitting. At fifteen going on sixteen, he was already six feet tall, and it seemed impossible that just a few months before, we had all but given up hope of pulling him away from gang friends. The dreadlocks and sullen attitude were gone. He still wasn't perfect, but for the most part he was hard-working, funny and agreeable. Coming close to dying can straighten out your priorities in a hurry.

"Are you heading back now?" he said.

"I am, indeed, or you'll miss breakfast *and* the bus."

He grinned. "You could let me drive the Jeep."

"As in *on your own* or as in *a licensed driver accompanying a cute kid with a learner's permit*?"

"Either way is good."

"Race me back and we'll see."

"I need to ask you something first."

My hands, busy untying the line, were stilled by the tone in his voice. "Are you in trouble, Davis?"

"Not me, but you could say a friend is, and I wonder if you could talk to her."

"Girlfriend?"

He shook his head. "She's just a friend from school. You have to promise not to tell Sheriff Council her name."

"Sure, I'll talk to her, Davis, but I don't want to make a promise here that wouldn't be in her best interest. I'll tell you what. Give me a run-down without a name and let's see what I think. Does that seem fair?"

His hesitation gave me a clue that she wasn't just any friend.

He took a deep breath and said, "She was somewhere she shouldn't have been last night…with somebody she wasn't supposed to be with."

So far, it didn't sound all that unusual for a teen. "You, Davis?"

He looked so shocked I believed him.

"No, not me! Another guy ran off and left her alone in the dark, scared out of her head, and she can't tell her dad because she's afraid of what he might do if he hears she sneaked out of the house. She says he's real strict and kind of mean sometimes."

There was something about the way he kept looking at the saltwater lapping at the side of the boat.

A little shiver ran up my arm. "Tell me you aren't talking about the two Arboretum murders night before last?"

"Yeah," he said.

"If they had anything—anything at all to do with the killings—then we need to let Stan hear right away."

"*She* didn't. I don't know the guy all that well, but she swears the two of them just stumbled over the bodies, and then the lily-livered jerk ran off and left her in the dark without even a flashlight."

I studied his worried face, filled with the confidence of youth that everything could be fixed. I wasn't his mother, but I remembered his baby arms around my neck when I, too, was only fifteen, which no doubt prompted the easy decision that I would live to regret.

Davis was doing the driving, and on the way to pick up Peggy Hollowell, I reached the conclusion that I'd lived a long life and might as well stop worrying about running into a ditch or the back of a gasoline tanker. From Bald Eagle Lane to Greenville Loop Road was no more than eight miles, but long before we arrived at her house, my right foot ached from trying to brake on the passenger side.

I had to wonder whether my own learner's permit had had the same effect on my father and Randolph. If it hadn't, the two men had been made of sterner stuff than I was. I tried hard not to shriek and lose face when he ran a red light at a major intersection during full morning traffic. The scariest part of all was looking months down the road when Davis would have his real permit. Self-preservation is in short supply at fifteen, and we were uneasy about what kind of driving to expect when he was allowed to have other teens along. I kept reminding myself that he was a great kid and was getting older and more mature with each passing day.

My bag was stowed in the back of the Jeep for the drive to Hillsborough, and it occurred to me that walking the hundred and seventy miles might beat riding with a teenage driver.

Peggy wasn't at all what I expected. She turned out to be a quiet, shy fifteen-year-old in faded jeans and a University of North Carolina sweatshirt. Because of her blonde hair, Davis commented that she looked enough like me to be my daughter.

"She could be," I said, giving him a stern-mother look, "if I had given birth when I was fifteen." In truth, unlike me, Peggy was little more than five feet tall with delicate features, a baby's mouth, and hair the color of fine Egyptian cotton in a long plait down her back. At five-foot-eight, no one has ever accused me of being delicate. As for a small mouth, well…it's better not to go there.

She answered our casual questions in a low voice that trailed away at the end of her sentences like dandelion seeds on a breeze. For some reason, I thought of Davis at ten, all of five years ago, yelling as my boat passed under the Wrightsville Beach drawbridge just for the sheer joy of hearing the echoing bounce of sound.

I wasn't sure this girl had ever been loud enough to cause an echo and wondered what could have happened in her young life to make her so timid.

In front of Laney High School, I said to Davis, "Why don't you go ahead while we talk girl-talk for a few minutes, assuming that's OK with Peggy."

It was clear he wanted to stay, but he was a good kid at heart, and when she nodded, he got out of the Jeep without so much as a hurt look.

"Come up front then, Peggy, so I won't get a crick in my neck," I said, and she climbed in beside me with a backpack so big I wondered how she walked with the weight of it.

"Davis tells me you're a straight-A student."

"Yes, ma'am," she said.

"He also says you might want to talk to me a little. Is that right?"

"Yes, ma'am. Because you know the sheriff and all, and I can't tell him myself."

"I'm glad to talk to you, sweetie, but I'm in a tricky spot here. This is something your parents should be doing, and I don't want to make things worse for you by…well, I guess *interfering* is the word they would use."

"There's just my dad," she said with a little catch in her voice. "I could have told my mom, but she died last year."

Well, I had my explanation for the lost, vulnerable look in her eyes.

I chose my words carefully. "That's a hard thing to deal with. My own mother died when I was fourteen, a sailing accident, and nothing was ever the same again."

I thought I saw a faint glint of tears.

"Davis told me. He said that's why you would understand."

"What happened with *your* mother?"

"You wouldn't…" She stopped and stared out the side window where the treetops were turning yellow and red with the season. "She fell down the stairs and hit her head. I stayed with her for a week in the hospital, but I don't think she ever knew I was there."

"What was her name?"

"Lynn—the same as my middle name."

"Mine was Sylvia," I said. "You've been through a bad time, haven't you?"

"Yes, ma'am," she whispered, clutching the backpack to her chest like a shield. "It's hard on my dad, too. He still writes letters to her sometimes."

"He must be lonely without her. It probably helps him cope."

She nodded.

"Is Davis a good friend?"

"Yes, ma'am. He's the best."

"Just friends? No romance there?"

Like Davis when I'd asked him the same question, she reacted with surprise. "We don't think of each other that way, and besides, my dad would have a heart attack if he knew we were even friends. It shouldn't bother him that Davis is black, but he's like that, you know. I don't think he can change."

I nodded. "Some people can't. What does your dad do?"

"He's a minister."

"That's good, isn't it? He must be a very understanding person."

She shrugged. "I guess. When he's feeling OK. But he wouldn't like me knowing Davis, nor would my grandparents and all the aunts and uncles on my dad's side. My mother was different, though. I could talk to her about almost anything."

"Like the Arboretum Monday night?"

She rested her chin on the backpack, looking straight ahead, nervous fingers picking at loose threads. "Yes, ma'am, like that."

"Peggy?"

She gazed at me with eyes so young and innocent, I felt as old as Methuselah, and had to remind myself that this baby had tiptoed out of the house in the dark of the night to be with a boy.

"Tell me what you want me to know. I promise not to judge you."

She took a quick, deep breath, as if eager to give away the information to someone else. "I shouldn't have sneaked out of the house, but I let Kevin convince me that my dad wouldn't find out, and he was so...you know..."

"I was a teenager once."

Her cheeks reddened, but there was little defiance in her voice. "It's my fault. I wanted to go. He said he only wanted to kiss me, but I knew better." She studied nails bitten to the quick for an extended moment before continuing. "It was dark as a bat cave and I kept tripping over things because I wouldn't let him turn on the flashlight until we got onto the Arboretum grounds. But he didn't seem to care, even when I snagged my new jacket on the fence."

She paused as if realizing none of that mattered.

"Go on," I said. "Did you see or hear anything out of the ordinary?"

"Can I borrow a cigarette? My dad would have a hissy if he knew, but he smokes cigars a lot. I hate that."

I shook my head, wondering if she was stalling, nervous, or both. "I don't smoke." *And wouldn't give one to a kid if I did.* "You were about to tell me whether you heard anything."

"Was I?" She faltered. "Some kind of animal in the leaves. I thought it was a deer or a big dog, but Kevin said that was stupid, that deer couldn't get into the Arboretum. It was only after I read about it in the paper that I thought it might have been whoever killed those two people. Do you think it was?"

"Probably not," I lied to keep her from having nightmares. "It could have been one of the raccoons. The killer would have been long gone by the time you arrived. Count on it. And then…?"

"I was sorry I went with Kevin way before we got to the teahouse. Mad at him, too, because I was nervous about snakes and spiders and he kept pawing me like an immature jerk. I guess…we smelled them first, before we knew they were there, I mean, and we couldn't see anything because it was so dark. I made Kevin turn on the flashlight."

"What then?" I said.

She shivered in the warm Jeep. "There was blood, and I thought… I don't know what I thought. I'd never seen a body before except in a funeral home, and they just looked…dead."

"Did you touch anything?"

"No, of course not." She looked at me as if I'd lost my mind.

"So what did you do?"

Long eyelashes closed tightly together, moist and bare of any trace of makeup. She looked more like eleven than fifteen, wringing her hands in front of Laney High instead of elementary school, as if the bus had dropped her off at the wrong place.

"Kevin dropped the flashlight."

I reached for her hand as she began to tremble. "It's all right, Peggy. You don't have to go on."

"I do! I have to tell *somebody*."

"OK," I said, beginning to wonder if she needed more help than a sympathetic ear. "Go on."

"Everything happened really fast," she said in a rush. "The light went out and it was so pitch dark—blacker than I could ever have imagined—and I got turned around and couldn't find the doorway, couldn't see anything, couldn't find Kevin. I couldn't *breathe* I was so scared."

"What was Kevin doing?"

"Running away," she said in a little explosion of anger. "He ran and left me all alone in the dark with dead bodies, the dirty coward."

"Panic does strange things to people, even adults." I knew because I had been there a time or two myself. "But I agree it was a cowardly thing to do."

She nodded. "The worst. Even when I got outside I couldn't see much better. I couldn't find the bridge and finally fell in the rock pool. It was the Japanese fence that helped me figure out where I was. After that, I climbed over and ran through back yards until I got home. All I could think was that something was still behind me, and I didn't know what or who."

"Fear and panic," I said. "Scary stuff." I remembered the heart-pumping, paralyzing terror that still haunted me in my dreams.

She glanced down at her hands again before looking at me. "And then I was just scared to death my dad would hear me sneaking in the back door. Do you think those people might have still been alive? That if I had called the police…?"

"Not likely," I said, thinking about what I'd seen in the teahouse. "The wounds would have been too severe."

The shrill bell was deafening in the crisp fall air. Peggy jumped and scrambled for the door handle. "I've got to run or I'll be late. Remember, my dad can't ever find out what happened. Promise you won't tell the sheriff my name or Kevin's."

I didn't answer fast enough and she clutched at my sleeve, suddenly realizing her fate was in the hands of a stranger about whom she knew nothing except what Davis had told her.

"I would be in so much trouble I can't even *begin* to tell you."

"Peggy…"

"Promise me!"

"All right." I gave in to her fierce anxiety.

"Oh, thank you, thank you, thank you." She embraced me before scrambling out of the Jeep as if the backpack weighed two pounds instead of thirty and the weight of the world had been lifted from her small shoulders.

"One last question." I grabbed her backpack strap. She turned.

"What happened to the flashlight?" I said, and watched her go pale, realizing that police might trace the object first to Kevin's door and then to hers. She started to speak, then turned and ran like a young gazelle up the sidewalk, disappearing through the heavy doors without looking back.

Well done, Davenport, I thought. *You just scared the hell out of a kid who was traumatized already.*

I sat for a moment thinking, or trying to, about how much to tell Stan Council without revealing the source. It would mean choosing my words with extra care. He was smarter than your average bear, and was going to be about as happy as an aging grizzly to hear I was withholding information.

The Jeep was already in gear and my foot on the accelerator when I looked up to see a man standing at the front bumper, staring in through the windshield, making no attempt to get out of the way. Because of the gray three-piece suit he wore, my first guess was that he might be the principal. I raised my hand in a small wave.

Five seconds passed. I counted them.

After a little tap on the horn, he still neither moved nor blinked. I opened the car door and got out.

"Is there a problem?" I said.

He waited a beat too long, like one of those live CNN interviews from Uzbekistan or Bangladesh. Instead of answering, he turned his back and walked away toward the school entrance.

It seemed a curious way to discourage visitors. Annoying and strange, but no doubt effective.

Chapter Five

I make so many phone calls while driving that the Jeep might as well be designated an office. This saves me a substantial amount of time that would otherwise be spent twiddling my thumbs at red lights around town. On the way to Wrightsville Beach, Stan Council was third on the list.

"Where are you?" he said.

"In the Jeep, heading to the beach jobs. After that I'm driving to Hillsborough. Isabella Vitelli died yesterday morning."

"Ah," he said. "I'm sorry to hear that, but from what you've told me, it might be a blessing."

"It would be hard to argue with you on that one. Still…" I couldn't quite find the words. Isabella had suffered badly with cancer for the last few years.

"I know what you're trying to say, so I won't try to talk you out of going, but are you sure you want to get mixed up in that crowd again?"

By *that crowd*, he meant my father-in-law, Sam Vitelli, who was somehow involved in organized crime. Exactly how, I didn't know or want to know. He had been good to me through the years when Daniel destroyed himself, so I tried not to dwell on his occupation. We never discussed it when we talked, and I didn't think about it much anymore beyond the occasional nightmare about his son's murder.

"Some things have to be done, Stan. I owe Isabella that much. It's been years since I left New York. With luck, no one will even recognize me at the funeral."

He grunted. "Why Hillsborough instead of New York?"

"Sam has a farm west of Durham in Orange County. She loved it enough to want to be buried there."

"Make sure you keep that cell phone charged and with you at all times. Does your grandma know where you're going?"

"Of course."

"What did she say?"

"The same thing you did. Keep the cell phone handy."

"If you're determined to go, that's the best and only advice I can give you. You're not going to listen anyway."

"Well, thank you," I said, "but that wasn't why I called. I have information for you, without being able to explain anything about the source."

He went quiet for a moment. "The Burris murders? This better be something you heard by accident—not information you snooped around to get."

"I was minding my own business, as usual."

He made sounds resembling snorted laughter.

"Stan…"

"Go ahead. I'm listening."

"A couple of teenagers sneaked out after midnight to meet in the teahouse and wound up getting the scare of their lives. The boy dropped the flashlight and ran, leaving the girl to find her own way out in the dark. She's terrified her father will find out about it and made me promise I wouldn't give you her name."

Stan said, "How the *devil* did you get involved?"

"I can't really tell you that, either, except to say it was through a friend of a friend. But her fear seems genuine—enough anyway to keep her from slipping out the back door in the dark for a while."

"She'd better be afraid. Whoever did this knew what he was doing. I'd hate to think we had a professional hit man in town—or worse. What if the murders are gang-related and those two are involved?"

"No," I said. "She's sweet and innocent, the way girls were fifty years ago. She made me promise—not once but twice, and without the promise I wouldn't have anything at all to tell you."

"You haven't told me much, except that two kids probably trampled all over the crime scene." I could hear fingers drumming on his desk, a habit he had when he was thinking hard.

I waited.

"I don't like this. Those kids could be guilty as all get out or know who the murderer is. So you aren't going to tell me the boy's name or who she is? If we don't question them, how...?"

"Stan, she's fifteen. Why would she ask me to talk to you if she's guilty?"

"You'd think that makes a difference, wouldn't you? The truth is, I've learned not to trust even the young ones. You're not getting off so easy. I may have to bear down hard before it's over. But for now, get me their shoes, all four of them. We've got a dandy print where somebody stepped in blood, and if it belongs to some kid, at least we won't be chasing down rabbit holes for weeks trying to match it. And find out if she can remember hearing or seeing anything else. Can you do that as soon as you get back here? And when will that be?"

"Late tomorrow, Thursday. And yes I can."

"OK. Good. Now promise me something else."

"What?"

"That if anybody in Hillsborough so much as breathes funny, you call me on the spot."

I would remember much later that I laughed and said, "Of course. No problem with *that*."

Harbor Island sits between two channels, one of which connects it to the beach on the east, and the other to the mainland west of the drawbridge. Officially it's part of the town of Wrightsville Beach.

I turned down a sleepy street overhung with live oaks and found my construction supervisor up to his backside in alligators, even that early in the morning. A team of Brooklyn painters, all brothers, were having a shouting match in the front yard. As if that weren't enough, exasperated tile men were insisting that *no way in hell had they arrived with the wrong tiles*, and two state inspectors were standing firm that we couldn't so much as pull a nail from the old pier without a CAMA permit. The dock builders were not amused. I had little sympathy. They knew better than to proceed without the right paperwork, but were probably cutting corners because their own boss hadn't been around to quarterback.

And it wasn't even Monday morning.

Jinks Farmer, who looked as if he'd dragged himself to the job from a heavy date the night before, was relieved to see me. He had a degree in Sociology, but had worked construction for a couple of years and been my supervisor since March. He had a fine eye for detail and a good manner with the clients, but better than that, he was a stickler for making sure we got a quality job from every sub. Once upon a time, he'd been sweet on me until he got to know me well enough to find someone with a more adoring temperament. As friends, we got along well most of the time, which was a good thing since problems were a daily, sometimes hourly, occurrence on a job.

I put two fingers to my mouth and gave a piercing whistle, the way Randolph had taught me when I was ten. An instant hush fell over the groups.

As much as it stung my ego, I had long suspected it didn't hurt to have blonde hair and long legs. Hopefully, character, talent, and a good work ethic last a lot longer than looks. So far I'd had no problems being successful in the construction business, but it remained to be seen whether I would have the same influence at sixty as thirty. I didn't have to whistle very often.

"Gentlemen," I said, "we have elderly neighbors on either side of this project. Do you think we can get this sorted out before the Wrightsville police get here?" I turned to the inspectors. "Barry, the ink is only just dry on the CAMA. I'm sorry for the confusion, but Jinks didn't know, and we don't want to hold you up this morning." I slid the permit copy from my clipboard and handed it over.

Rule number one on a construction site says every sub's time is as valuable as our own. Rule number two says we avoid confrontations with inspectors no matter what the cost.

"Regulations tell you to keep it posted." Barry handed it back and jerked his thumb toward the sign at the road, feet already moving toward his truck. He was new, a stickler for crossing and dotting every "t" and "i" without spending more than three minutes at each site.

I nodded with the kind of smile necessary when confronting inspectors who have the power to make or break a project with delays if you piss them off. A lot of inexperienced builders discover this the hard way. Some of them are no longer in the business.

"Absolutely," I said. "Within minutes…and both of you have a nice day."

By then I was talking to his back.

"Asshole," Jinks muttered under his breath. "Like I didn't tell him the same thing."

I flashed him a look and moved on to Lester Perry, who had worked for my father and run the best tile-laying business in southeastern North Carolina for thirty years.

"Lester, you handsome old son of a gun. I haven't seen you in months. What seems to be the problem?"

He took the toothpick out from between tobacco-stained teeth and held out his hand. "Well, sugar," he drawled, giving me the invoice, "seems like we got ourselves a little mix-up. The tiles we were given ain't the right ones, at least according to your foreman here, and I figure only the boss is gonna know for sure what to do if we're getting started any time today."

I did a quick three-way check between the information stamped on the side of the boxes, his invoice, and mine. "Looks like you won't be going fishing today, Lester. This order is right on the money. Sorry for the confusion, and it's my fault, because I changed the color of the tile late yesterday without telling Jinks. You be nice to him, you hear? He looks like he had a late night."

"Anything you say, ladyboss." Lester guffawed, winked twice, and spat tobacco juice in the sand. "Come on boys, let's get to work. What you standing around for? We ain't got all day."

Over my shoulder, I saw Jinks roll his eyes. Now if

only the hot-tempered Ruggiero brothers would be so easy. The dock builders were still lolling around, no doubt hoping there would be at least one fistfight to liven things up a bit. With few exceptions—and I was hoping this wouldn't be one of them—life is not exciting on construction sites.

"OK, fellows," I said. "The show is over. Time for you to get wet." I made shooing motions with my hands, the kind of thing female bosses can get away with most of the time. It didn't speed them up much, but they ambled away in the general direction of the dock.

The oldest painter was Danny, but I could never remember the names of the other two. The three looked enough alike, plump and balding early, that I was always tempted to refer to each of the younger ones as the *other brother Danny*, but I didn't dare. To a man they had no sense of humor—not a scrap between them—and took umbrage at the slightest inflection that might indicate disrespect. On the plus side, they were fast, perfectionist painters.

"Brothers," I said. "Sorry to leave you till last, but I knew your problem must be crucial. What's wrong?"

The three began talking at once about missing paint. As usual, everything was spoken at the top of their voices, as if they had grown up vying for attention by trying to out-shout one another. Like a kindergarten teacher, I held up a hand.

Miraculously, they stopped.

"Danny, will you explain?"

He scowled toward Jinks. "I've told him twice in the last week that our equipment is disappearing, including five-gallon buckets of paint. He keeps blowing me off. I think he's the one stealing it or knows who is, and I'm not about to work on a job where the foreman steals my stuff."

One of the baby Dannys interrupted. "And I'm telling you it's that snot-nosed kid in the big yellow house. I've seen him slinking around twice late in the day, but big brother here always knows better than anybody else."

Closer to Jinks' age and not to be outdone, the third brother raised his voice about fifty decibels above the others. "And I'm sick of the both of you yammering on from sunup to sundown about the damn equipment and paint. I'll say it one more time. *Nothing is missing!* I was the last one working yesterday, and I should know. You're paranoid about the goddamn paint."

"You ungrateful little piece of shit," Danny said. "I ought to kick your thankless ass."

"Whoa!" I raised my own voice, wondering what I would do if they actually came to blows. "Let's all calm down here. This is a residential neighborhood with children and old ladies, so watch your language. Now, while I can't say whether anything is missing, I am certain of one thing. Jinks is not involved. It's a given, so just put that idea aside. This is the first I've heard about anything being missing since we started this job, so someone tell me exactly what it is and…"

"It wouldn't be the first time a foreman was stealing from a job," Danny said.

"And it won't be the last. But Jinks isn't responsible, so what do we need to do? Reimburse you, padlock a room, take the supplies home, or all of the above? We want the same thing here—to do a good job on time, collect our money, and move on to the next one. The Ruggieros are the best. That's why I keep hiring you."

Ah, the magic words had been uttered. As usual, after going off like firecrackers and fizzling just as fast, they seemed mollified. I wondered how their mother had stood it when the three of them were teenagers in the same house. Mom had lived with them when they first moved to Wilmington. After six months, she'd remarried and moved to far-away California.

I couldn't imagine why.

Just when I thought everything was calm, Danny's testosterone kicked in again. He pointed a finger at Jinks and said, "We lose any more stuff and I'm going to punch your lights out."

What the hell is it with men? A quick look at Jinks was enough to convince me that I had to do something quickly or four grown men would need a tetanus booster. There was no way the baby Dannys would stay out of the fray.

What the world really needs is more estrogen.

I stepped between them, fast, and laughed, trying to play it light. "Well doggone it, Danny. I hope not, because then—whether Jinks deserved it or not—when he'd finished with you, I'd have to call you an ambulance, fire you, and have you arrested all at the same time. After that, I'd have to pay all the medical bills for Jinks and find new painters. Doesn't sound like it's worth it to me. What do you say? Can we get back to work now?"

For the time being anyway, Danny gave way grudgingly with a heavy last glare at Jinks, spitting on the ground and scratching himself in private, baseball-player places—two things I'd yet to see a woman do on a construction site.

By the time I'd checked on two other jobs at the beach, it was later than I thought, my watch reading ten-forty as I crossed the Wrightsville Beach drawbridge. I cut across to Oleander Drive and on toward downtown Wilmington, pulling into my grandmother's driveway a little after eleven.

The house was a two-story of Italianate design, built by my great-great-grandfather with cotton money at a time when sailing ships made regular rounds between Wilmington, London, and Nassau.

Lurking in the garage were two monster cars, a Cadillac and a Lincoln, both of which were more than ten years old. I worried about the consequences of breakdowns and broached the subject of a newer car from time to time. It wasn't as if Gran couldn't afford a fleet of Bentleys if she wanted them. Whether it was the new technology or depression-era frugality, I was informed each time I brought it up that it wasn't my business—in a Southern ladylike way, of course. It was just as well. A GPS system might take ten years off my grandmother's life.

They weren't expecting me, but seemed to love it when I dropped by without calling ahead. It wasn't garden club, bridge, or grocery day, so I pretty much knew where to find them. The routine never varied. Coffee was at eleven o'clock, lunch at one, dinner at seven.

I went up the back stairs and found Gran and Lucille on the porch watching two bright yellow kayaks glide down the Cape Fear River. As well as I could tell, the discussion centered around what nimble legs and arms they had once had and whether they would have the nerve to try kayaking if they were forty years younger.

They'd both come close to drowning last spring in that same dark, fast-moving water. I thought the fact that they could even consider being out on the river again must mean there weren't too many post-traumatic scars.

The wicker table by the door held a silver tray with enough homemade cookies and cakes to fatten a small family of pigs, so they must have known I was coming.

My two silver-haired ladies were as thin as wet stockings on a clothesline.

They both tried to act surprised, although I knew full well that Randolph must have called and told them I'd stop by on my way out of town.

"May I join the party?" I kissed my grandmother on the cheek and hugged Lucille just to devil her.

I've had a wary relationship with Lucille since my early teens. She's devoted to Eleanor Monroe and has been for almost five decades. My wayward youth is the reason she holds a grudge, and I've often thought she must keep a list somewhere of every transgression that caused my grandmother grief. I've watched how she treats Davis and my five-year-old niece, so I know she must have been more demonstrative toward me when I was little, but I don't remember it. She possesses a sharp tongue, and I'm careful around her, although the temptation to pester her is always there.

My grandmother said, "We were hoping you'd drop by before you left town. I was sorry to hear about Isabella Vitelli."

"Thank you. I'm afraid it's one of those times when I don't quite know whether to feel sad or relieved that she won't have to endure more pain. In many ways, she was a lot like you. I'm sorry you didn't get to know her."

Lucille said, "I made a coconut cake for you to take with you. Be sure you don't forget it."

Food is Lucille's remedy for just about everything, a Southern approach to psychology that often works better than two-hundred-dollar sessions. A compassionate ear, cholesterol-laden food—it's a wonder the two of them weren't as fat as figs.

"What a thoughtful thing to do. Thank you, Lucille."

"You look nice," she said. "Is that a new skirt? I was beginning to think those jeans were permanently glued to your backside."

Gran took a cup from her hand. "Don't tease her, Lucille. She might have a wreck on her trip, and wouldn't you feel bad then?"

I winked at the woman who treated my grandmother like a saint. "I'm a very good driver. Maybe I'll even buy a new dress before I get back."

"Red," they said in unison.

I swear older women lead vicarious lives. If I came home with a dress of any color, they'd be sure to suspect a man somewhere and want all the details. At the rate I was going, they might fall over in a permanent snooze before there was anything to tell.

"The main reason I came by, Gran, was to make sure there were no aftershocks from yesterday."

"Gracious, no. I've seen plenty of dead people in my life, and no doubt there'll be more. Word has already gotten out that Senator Burris was cheating on his wife. Those poor, poor children. I always feel sorriest for the families."

Lucille put her feet up on a footstool, something she would have been too proud to do ten years ago.

"It's going to be a big funeral—at least five hundred people. When I die, I want to be floated down this old river on a burning funeral pyre with loads of flowers and a thousand people lining the banks. Remember that when the time comes, Eleanor."

I had to smile at the image. The numbers were about right and she deserved it, but the state environmental authorities might have other ideas.

"When did you decide that?" Gran asked.

Women their age talk a lot about funerals. The music, the flowers, the casket, all seemed to become more interesting with each passing year. I listened to them chatter like sisters while their plates remained untouched. They stayed thin by forgetting to eat.

When there was a lull, I remembered my promise to Davis and asked, "Do either of you know a Reverend Hollowell here in town?"

Lucille wrinkled her nose. "I don't know anything about holyroller preachers."

"Is that what he is?" I asked.

"I don't think I know him," Gran said. "There was a Hollowell who ran off with a married Watkins girl, but that was years ago."

"How many years?" I asked.

"Oh, honey, it must have been forty at least."

I shook my head. "It has to be the wrong Hollowell. This one has a small church on Market Street called Church of the Faithful or something like that. Does it ring a bell?"

Gran shook her head. "Lucille?"

"I don't know enough to tell it honestly, but I hear it's a very strict church, the kind where women are expected to be obedient and keep their mouths shut. It wouldn't suit me at all. I always say that if God seriously intended a literal interpretation of the Bible, we'd all be pillars of salt."

My grandmother raised her eyebrows. "Not me."

Lucille opened her mouth and closed it again. As devoted as she was to Gran, I was willing to bet there were juicy, untold stories that would go to the grave with both of them.

Gran said between sips of tea, "You must have a reason for asking about the Reverend."

"There's a young girl I know who told Davis her father was mean to her. I don't know what that implies beyond being a strict parent, and she's given him good reason for that. I'm not really concerned, but would you put out a few feelers at bridge club to see if anything pops up? Don't make a big deal out of it, though. If Davis finds out, he'll have a conniption."

I left soon afterward when the conversation turned to funeral outfits, content that all was well in the household, and wishing it could last for another lifetime.

Chapter Six

Interstate 40 begins at Wilmington, almost at the Atlantic Ocean, and on it you can travel west all the way to Barstow, California. I'd done it once by myself. It was a lot of miles, more than twenty-five hundred, and wasn't something I wanted to repeat without brilliant companionship. This time I wasn't going nearly so far.

I took the interstate through Raleigh and the Research Triangle, where, for once, the traffic was flowing. Near Efland, I doubled back onto US 70 and came in the back way, avoiding Hillsborough, skirting along the edge of Duke Forest.

Sam's farm lay west of Durham a few miles up NC 86 where the land began to roll like mellow English hills and valleys. Daniel and I spent our honeymoon at this farm, the best days before the storm that submerged me in a tide of grief, guaranteeing I would never be the same.

I turned up a drive that wound its way a quarter of a mile to the top of the hill where a three-storied house stood outlined by the blue October sky. It was old and not nearly so impressive as the estate in Westchester County, but before Sam bought it in the eighties, the same family had lovingly cared for every hand-made brick and column for more than a hundred and twenty-five years. The last of the Southern line died in his rocking chair on the front porch. There are worse ways to go.

The road was bordered by eastern red cedars, almost two feet in diameter, flanked by fields where Black Angus and Belted Galloway cattle lifted their heads in curiosity. Near the garage, a gleaming hearse with New York plates was parked alongside five other dark vehicles, including a black limo. None would have cost less than twice the sticker price of my Jeep.

My watch said four o'clock as I thumped the doorknocker twice and waited. I knocked a second time before finally opening the door and walking into the wide hallway that smelled of bayberry and funeral flowers.

"Hello," I called, the sound muffled by thick walls and high ceilings. And since it seemed beyond ill breeding to shout in a mourning household, I went looking for the source of raised voices—men's voices. As soon as I slid open one heavy wooden door to the library, four men standing in a cluster by the fireplace fell silent as if water pouring from a faucet had suddenly turned to ice. Something about the way they stood convinced me I'd interrupted an important conversation.

"I'm looking for Sam," I said. "Sorry to interrupt, but no one seemed to hear me."

Awkward seconds passed in which no one spoke, smiled, or moved a fraction of an inch in their dark suits. Three appeared to be in their fifties and sixties. The youngest, around forty, broke away from the group and crossed the room swiftly in expensive Italian shoes. He grasped my arm just above the elbow, propelling me back into the hallway and re-closing the sliding door.

"How did you get into this house?"

I pulled my arm away and myself up to my full height of five-foot-eight in flats. "I walked in."

"Don't try to be cute," he said. "Who allowed you inside?"

Allowed? I set my teeth at the tone in his voice.

"No one. The door was unlocked, and when my knock went unanswered, I turned the knob and let myself in. Now, if you don't mind, I'd like to see Sam, please."

"But I do mind! You can't barge into a private house…"

"Would you like me to wait outside on the doorstep while you call him? I have to warn you ahead of time, though, he isn't going to like it much."

Arthur Weiss hadn't yet recognized me, but once we left the dimly lit hallway, it wasn't going to take him long. I knew him immediately, in spite of the fact that his hair was now trimmed in a fashionable buzz cut to hide graying at the temples. He wore small gold-framed glasses that should have aged him, but instead added an air of distinction.

He was my dead husband's first cousin, the son of Sam Vitelli's sister. For most of the time I'd been a Vitelli, Arthur was away at Harvard earning advanced degrees in economics or finance. I could never recall which. What I could remember was that I had found him stuffy and condescending. Apparently, he hadn't changed.

Seven years is a long time, and life goes on. I hadn't seen him since Daniel was murdered when I was twenty-three and very much a different person. Life has a way of knocking you down from time to time. If you get back up at all, you're changed. Now my hair was pulled back into a loose French twist, and I had lost that uncertainty of youth where the Arthurs of this world had any effect on me at all.

I was tired of playing games. "I'm Carroll. Daniel's widow."

He let his breath out in a sound that was half relief, half hiss. "I didn't recognize you."

"No," I said. "I didn't think so."

"What are you doing here?"

"The same as you, Arthur. Because of Isabella and Sam."

He seemed disconcerted, as if he was having difficulty remembering Isabella had just died, as if he'd forgotten there was to be a funeral. He ran a hand over his cropped head, glanced toward the parlor door.

"Neither of them so much as mentioned your name to me for years. You dropped off the face of the earth, Singapore or somewhere like that. I got the distinct impression they never wanted to see you again after what happened to Daniel."

"Why would you think that? I did travel for several years, but I've been back in the real world, living my own life for quite a long while now. Even from overseas, we kept in touch. Why wouldn't we?"

He had been caught off balance, but there was only a hint of anger in his eyes before he nodded, the civilized mask slipping back across his face.

I wondered why Sam hadn't told him we talked often, and if that meant he didn't trust him.

Over Arthur's shoulder I saw one of the older men standing in the library doorway. I hadn't heard the door open, nor had Arthur, who turned when he saw me watching. A look passed between them.

Arthur said, "It's nothing. I'll be right there." The door closed again.

It isn't easy for a man in a thousand-dollar handmade suit to look skittish, but Arthur came close. He even opened the front door in an effort to hustle me away.

"We're in the middle of something. I need to get back. No doubt you'll find Sam in the gazebo down the hill, and if you're still around later, I'll talk to you then. Do you know how to get there?"

"I know where it is, so don't trouble yourself. And I'll be spending the night," I added just for the hell of it. He had always been too full of himself.

He wasn't pleased, and as I stepped backwards

over the doorsill, his jaw stiffened before he closed the front door in my face.

I went out into the late afternoon sun slanting across the porch, wondering what kind of threat I could be to Arthur Weiss after seven years, and yes, wondering about the other three men huddled in serious conversation without Sam.

On the other hand, when it comes to the Vitelli family, there are a lot of things a girl is better off not knowing.

Sam was sitting on a stone bench overlooking the small country cemetery begun sometime in the mid eighteen hundreds, watching two workmen put the finishing touches on a solitary gravesite.

I stopped for a moment to watch before he sensed my presence. It was a poignant scene, the kind of photograph *Life* magazine might have published once—an old man watching a grave being dug for his beloved wife. The sadness of it almost took my breath away.

I was struck by the fact that his hair was whiter, his shoulders smaller, almost hunched as he leaned on a wooden cane with both hands, more frail than I remembered. The years of Isabella's cancer had not been kind.

A cluster of cattle watched from under the kind of rounded oak that only grows where the dirt is rich and deep. In our sandy coastal soil, the same tree could grow a hundred years and never get an equivalent shape.

In the shade, the temperature dropped ten degrees. I wondered how long he had been sitting there.

"Sam?" I said.

He turned at the sound of my voice, a look on his face that said he'd been far away in another place, another time.

"Carroll." He smiled, exhaling a sigh of gladness as he gathered my hands in his cold fingers, kissed me slowly on both cheeks. "I did not think it was possible you could grow more beautiful. Isabella would be pleased. We missed you so, both of us. I cannot tell you how much."

"How are you, Sam?"

"Not bad, not bad, considering. I will hardly know how to breathe without her, but who could wish her another single day of pain in this life? It must be a sin to be so glad she will not have to suffer any longer."

"She felt like a mother to me, more than I could ever express, for all the years I knew her. After Daniel's death I barely saw her at all, you know, just once in Paris and again in San Francisco for a day. But she knew—she had to have known—how much I valued her."

He tightened his grip. "Never doubt it, not even for a minute. Your letters helped keep her going, especially this last year. I read them to her, often more than once, because they brought her joy just knowing how much your life was filled with family and contentment."

"What a kind thing to say." I had never told either of them about the nightmares, and kept my letters and calls light and filled with family incidents. Perhaps I had even exaggerated a little about how good life was.

"You were the daughter we always wanted and never had, you know. A daughter-in-law who loved us in return was like a miracle—even more so after Daniel died. It was not only my decision that we keep you physically separated from our lives. Isabella felt strongly that the risk was too great, but perhaps she never told you."

"Not a word."

"You probably should not be here now."

"I'll stay somewhere else tonight if you want me to, but I need to be here tomorrow for the service. Then I'll go. I promise."

"No," he said. "Stay at the house tonight. You will be safer here than alone somewhere. Arthur will keep an eye out."

Not likely, I thought.

We were quiet for a few moments. Sam's eyes were fixed on the digging men as if his personal supervision were the last, most precious thing he could do for Isabella.

In a sudden gust, the wind blew sweetgum leaves

around our feet, settled them on our shoulders in a mantle of autumn fragrance. We never got the rich colors on the coast.

A car backfired somewhere down by the main road, breaking the tranquility. The taller of the two diggers paused with his shovel in mid-air.

Even then the danger didn't register.

Sam's hands were like ice. "When they're finished, we need to get you back to the house for a warm drink."

He nodded. "She loved this farm. I'm glad I decided to bring her here."

Another backfire sounded, louder, closer. Sam raised his head, a surprised look on his face.

The workman was running in our direction, shouting, "Get on the ground! Get down!"

Sam half rose to his feet, dropped his cane, and went down on one knee.

I'm a slow learner. It took a sound like an axe chop thudding into the tree next to me before I realized that someone was shooting at us.

Or at Sam. Or at me.

By then the workman had reached the bench where we were sitting, pushing us down, my face into the grass, falling on top of me. I felt the breath leave my chest in a whoosh as the bench toppled over on the three of us.

"Goddamn it," Ben Satterwhite said. "Don't you know shooting when you hear it?"

Chapter Seven

I couldn't have spoken if I'd wanted to. I was shocked and winded—literally and figuratively.

I blinked hard and opened my mouth to pull in air.

"Just stay down," Ben said.

Air at last filled my lungs as I tried to speak and looked into clear green eyes close to mine. He placed a finger across my lips for the barest of seconds before moving it away. I opened my mouth, closed it, and tried again as he gave a negative headshake.

"Are you hurt?"

I took another deep breath of air, feeling a relief so great I almost cried out. "Check on Sam," was all I could manage.

"Mr. Vitelli, are you hit?"

Another shot struck the corner of the bench and whined away like the sound effects in an old Western movie, sending stone chips flying. Three people made themselves as small as possible, while somewhere up the hill near the house voices were shouting.

Sam looked down at the hand covering his upper thigh where blood soaked a six-inch diameter of gray trousers and seemed surprised to find red stains on his fingers.

"Son of a bitch," he said with an anger I had seldom heard in his voice. Gone was the grieving widower, stooped and despondent. His expression said someone was going to pay dearly for this. To Ben Satterwhite he said, "And who the hell are you?"

"Jason Ellwood, Parker Funeral Services."

Sam looked from *Jason* to me. God knows what he read in my face, but I was still too shaken to hide much. "Well, Mr. Jason Ellwood, do you know anything about this?"

The wooded area to our left began to sound like a war zone, with firing coming from what seemed like three different directions.

"No, and keep your head down. I know enough to pray the automatic weapons I'm hearing are on our side."

"They damned well better be."

The last of the salvo echoed across the valley as running feet reached us. Arthur Weiss, gun in hand, was first on the scene. *Jason* was already out from under the bench and on his feet, his shovel swinging in a hard, fast arc. It connected with a ringing thud of metal on metal, sending the gun flying twenty-five or thirty feet into the meadow.

I had enough sense left to be impressed until I realized there were three other guns pointed in his direction.

"Hold it, hold it!" Sam said to the men I'd seen in the library. "What the hell do you think you're doing? Put the guns away. Arthur, get this damn bench off me."

"I think my hand is broken."

"Then get Johnny. Where the devil is he anyway?"

"Here, Boss. They got away, but I got a good look at the license plate." Johnny Rinaldi was a man in his middle forties, out of breath from running and an extra fifty pounds that had once been muscle. He was carrying a bazooka-barreled weapon unlike anything I had seen before—bigger than a revolver and shorter than a sawed-off shotgun. He looked from Arthur to *Jason*'s raised shovel, at the three other guns still in evidence.

"Who's this? Is he one of them, Boss?"

Sam took a deep breath. "He works for the funeral service. Now put the guns away, all of you, and get this damned rock off of us."

One by one, in reluctant slow motion, they slid the weaponry somewhere inside their jackets or coats, with Johnny going last. Only then did *Jason* put down the shovel and help lift the mammoth bench back in place. It took four of them, one lifting each corner, to do the job.

As I got to my feet, Johnny's jaw dropped in surprise. "Carroll?"

"Hello, Johnny. You'd better help Sam. I think he's been shot."

So Sam hadn't told anyone that I was coming to Hillsborough, not even Johnny who guarded him like the Swiss guards watch over the Pope.

"Don't make a fuss," Sam said. "It's only a flesh wound from a chip—not a bullet."

"You can't know that," I said, but Johnny was already cutting his trouser leg with a knife to make sure.

He sat back on his considerable haunches with relief. "Looks like you're right."

Arthur was still holding his right hand with an angry, shocked expression. The fingers were red and swollen. When I tried to take a look, I got a snarl for my concern.

"I said they're broken," he snapped. "And this man, whatever the hell you called him, is going to wish he'd never been born when I can use them again. I'll have his job for starters."

Sam, on his feet and supported by Johnny, said, "You will get your temper under control right now, Arthur, and that is *all* you will do. His quick thinking saved our lives and he deserves my gratitude, if not yours. He had no way of knowing that you were on our side."

I had one of those quick flashes I get from time to time, like words in my head so clear they can give me goose bumps and keep me awake at night. A psychiatrist friend once called it *intuitive reasoning based on analysis of expression, body language, and tone of voice*—a fancy way of saying I simply know it. The information is garbage a lot of the time. Often I get nothing at all when I need it most. There's no halo or bright light, just a kind of certainty, and it can make me cautious and edgy when it happens.

This time I got the distinct words, *no he isn't.* They

caused me to look at Arthur in a whole new light.

"I'll drive you to the emergency room," I said. "Mr. Ellwood can come with us and pay the bill."

The prospect of being in the same car with a gravedigger didn't seem to suit him. "Like hell I…"

"Arthur!" Sam glanced from me to Ben Satterwhite and back again. "That is an excellent idea. What do you say, Ellwood?"

He shrugged and scratched at the side of his chin. "The company will have the last word, of course. My partner can finish up here. Just let me have a word with him." He nodded to Sam, picked up his shovel, and strode back across the grass to where the partner was still standing behind the digging equipment. He talked for a few seconds before glancing at his watch and taking out a cellphone.

The oldest of the three library men, the one with a serious five o'clock shadow, said, "Are you sure you're OK, Sam? I think we should all get up to the house and out of the open. You don't want to be caught here if they come back." The other two remained silent.

Sam was watching Ben pick up something from the grass, and said, "Yes, of course. We can all use a drink. Johnny, where's my cane?"

It was hard not to notice that there was no talk of calling law enforcement. No talk of who *they* might be. All this would be discussed behind the library doors.

As they started back in a tight little knot, I said, "I'll wait for Ellwood. He seems more than capable of seeing me safely back. Give Arthur a drink and we'll be right behind you."

In unison they turned and looked at me, six pairs of male eyes that said they thought I had the hots for a gravedigger. I made my face as innocent as possible and gave them a little wave, trying not to think about what might happen if they found out Jason Ellwood was really Ben Satterwhite, former FBI agent.

Or maybe not so former.

When he was finished with his call, he came across the grassy hill and stood in front of me, very close, too damned close, in the same brown leather jacket I'd first seen him in. By then the others were out of sight and earshot.

"I thought you were dead," I said, realizing I was so angry it wasn't going to help much to count to ten.

"No. As you can see I'm very much alive."

"You could have let me know." There was a shrewish bite to my tongue that sounded like Lucille.

"No, I couldn't. When I can, I'll explain, but right now we don't want to arouse suspicions. You'll have to trust me."

"I did that. Look where it got me. Do you have any idea how it felt when I heard you'd been missing for two weeks?"

"Like the way I felt when Stan Council told me you were on your way to an organized crime reunion?"

"It's a funeral, damn it. For someone I cared an awful lot about."

He looked over my head at the house, not meeting my eyes. "Are we fighting here?"

"Yes."

"Because you know you're at a disadvantage with dirt on your face and skirt. Turn around."

"Forget the skirt. I'll take care of it. What difference does it make?"

He ignored me and began brushing at the back of my long skirt, his hands lingering. "Does this mean you take back all those sweet things you whispered in my ear a few weeks ago?"

I studied his bent head of Caribbean-bleached hair, the back of his neck as brown as pine bark, and didn't know whether to slap him or beg to be dragged into the nearby bushes. He looked up with a raffish grin that showed he knew exactly what I was thinking.

"You can take your hand off my backside now," I said.

He straightened and gave me a look that could have melted sand into glass. He had two weeks of grungy stubble on his chin and red mud all over the rest of him. In spite of his appearance, I almost wavered.

I turned and began walking toward the house. "But I don't even know you, do I, Mr. Jason Ellwood? So I won't be whispering anything at all in your ear or passing out privileges, now will I?"

He laughed, a low sexy sound that sent a tingle up my spine, and said, "God, I missed you."

Chapter Eight

A pissed-off Arthur was waiting at the foot of the front steps. His hand looked even more swollen, enough to give me a twinge of guilt for feeling only a small amount of sympathy. I regretted even that much as soon as he spoke.

He said to Ben, "You picked up my gun, so don't think you can get away with stealing it. Give it back, and if it's broken, you'll damned well pay for that, too."

Ben passed it to him without a word. The idea of a gun in Arthur's hand again made me more than a little uneasy. He looked it over on both sides and added, "You're wearing an expensive jacket for a gravedigger. You can't be making *that* much money. What did you say your name was?"

"Ellwood. Jason Ellwood." Ben glanced down at the worn leather with a careless shrug. "There's a second-hand store in Chapel Hill. I've been there once or twice."

Arthur frowned as if there was a lot more he wanted to say, but contented himself with, "Well, what are we waiting for?" He stalked to my Jeep and jerked the door open with his left hand. Ben got into the back seat behind him.

I drove down through the cedars to the main road while Arthur kept up a running spate of questions about where Ellwood was from, how long he'd worked for Parker Funeral, what kind of insurance they had. Things like that—all with a nasty attitude and the gun resting on his knee.

I waited for Ben to tell him to go to hell, but it never came. He answered in flat monotones, sitting forward on his seat so Arthur would have to turn all the way around to look at his face. He lived outside town down near the Eno River, had worked with Parker a few years, and he'd be sure and check about the insurance.

I kept my eyes on the rearview mirror and drove two miles to the local MEDAC. When Arthur fumbled for the door handle with the same hand that held the gun, I said, "There are laws in North Carolina against carrying concealed weapons. You'd better put the gun in the glove compartment before we go in."

He shot me a look that said *not a chance*, but at least slipped the gun in his pocket. I wondered who he distrusted the most—Ellwood, me, or the men back at the house. Maybe it was all of us.

In the waiting room, we sat on separate sofas while Arthur filled out the required paperwork. There was only a young mother with an infant ahead of him, but he wasn't pleased at even a ten-minute wait, sitting as far away as possible and scowling when the baby coughed or cried, which was often.

"Finally," he said to the nurse who came for him, causing her to roll her eyes as the door closed.

"With any luck," I said, "the gun will fall out of his jacket pocket, causing her to shoot him with it."

Ben laughed. "You're a hard-hearted woman, Ms. Davenport."

"Practical…just practical. You want a Coke, Mr. Ellwood? I'm buying if we can find a drink machine." We got up and checked with the receptionist, who pointed us down the hallway to an alcove near the stairway.

I fed dollar bills into the machine and handed him a Coke. "Arthur is up to something. I have no idea what, but I suspect it involves Sam, and he won't welcome either one of us getting in his way. Did you really need to give him back his gun?"

"There was a weapon aimed at his back the whole way here."

"You're kidding. I must have rocks for brains. The two of you in the same car with loaded guns? And I was wondering why I have this really bad feeling that something is about to happen."

In that condescending tone men use when humoring women, Ben said, "Are you saying you know something specific or is this one of your…ah …premonitions?"

I gave him *the look*. "Don't knock it. Right now for instance, I can sense you're about to make a chauvinist remark which could guarantee you a womanless, crusty bachelorhood into old age."

He put up both hands. "Then I bow to your

superior instincts and way with words. Did I tell you I missed you?"

"Yes, you did." I twisted the tab off my Coke can. "Now I'm wondering if you really meant it."

"Ah…" he said, putting his soft drink on top of the snack machine. "We can fix that."

"How?"

"Like this." He took the Coke out of my hand and placed it with his before pulling me into the stairwell where he proceeded to demonstrate, in a way that would have satisfied most of the female population, just how much he had missed me.

After long minutes, I wrapped my arms hard around his waist and leaned my head on his chest, tears not far away. "I thought you were dead. What are you doing here?"

"Shhh, babe, don't cry. Damn the Bahamian mail system, anyway. You can't believe I'd let you think I was dead if I could help it? You have my solemn word I sent a letter."

I thumped him on the chest with my open palm. "Your sister was in Wilmington Tuesday. Your own mother thinks you're dead. Couldn't you at least call her?"

"Not my mother, too?"

"Why else would your sister go searching for you in the Bahamas?"

"Which sister?"

"Mary."

He groaned. "That's a bad sign. Mary doesn't go off the deep end without good reason. It means my mother sent her. Shit. What a screw-up."

"I suppose you wrote Mrs. Satterwhite a letter, too?"

"Of course. What kind of son do you think I am? She wanted me to stay in touch every few days, and I promised her. I didn't particularly want to, but I did promise."

"So why a letter? There's always the telephone or e-mail."

He had a look of consternation on his face. "I couldn't. I didn't have my wallet, computer, cell phone, or even my watch."

Damned if I wasn't beginning to believe him. I took a deep breath. "So call your mother now."

He ran a hand tiredly through his hair. "I will. As soon as we're finished with Arthur. If I'm lucky, she won't have me buried for another hour."

I looked at him and waited.

"What?"

"Aren't you going to tell me just how you lost all your means of communication? Why you're here of all places?"

"It's a long story," he said. "We don't have the time."

I shook my head. "Did Stan send you?"

He chuckled. "In a way. Let's just say he was a big help. When I can, I'll explain everything. You'll laugh, I swear you will, but until that time, I'm asking you to trust me."

"Just this once." I gave him one of my best smiles, and he rewarded me with a hug that almost broke my ribs.

"That's my girl. Now, dry your eyes and do something with your mascara before Arthur gets even more suspicious."

"Not yet," I said. "I think I need more convincing."

He was easily inspired. I could have gone on being convinced for a lot longer, but he finished with a final press of his lips on my forehead—a reassuring, brotherly, unsatisfying kind of kiss. "If you want to get out of this stairwell without having your clothes torn off, you'd better go."

"Now *that* would singe Arthur's eyebrows."

We had recovered the drinks when he said in a cautious way, "There's one more thing."

"What?"

"I don't want you staying at Sam's house tonight. Don't even go inside. Just drop Arthur off and make an excuse. Any excuse."

I took a sip of Coke and then another. "Sam would never hurt me."

"I'm not worried about Sam. I'm worried about Arthur and Frank Foppiano for starters, not to mention Joseph Slagel and Luther Madigan—otherwise known as Mad Luther. Mind you, I haven't even gotten to whoever was taking potshots at you."

"Your point is a good one, but we don't know who's staying over at the house. Johnny Rinaldi is there, though, and Johnny watches over Sam like a wolf watches her pups."

"And who's going to watch out for Little Red Riding Hood?"

"That's another good point. What would you like me to do? Tell Sam I don't like the company he keeps? He already knows that, and has kept even our phone calls so quiet that Arthur hadn't heard my name mentioned in years. For all I know, he may have called a local motel himself and made a reservation for me."

"If so, that makes it easier."

"No, it doesn't. It still leaves Sam at the mercy of Arthur and the other three wolves."

"We're talking about the same person, right? Sam Vitelli? He's more than capable of taking care of himself."

"Normally, yes. I've never seen him like this, though, even when Daniel was murdered. It feels like…"

"Like what?"

"Like it's a bad time to abandon an old friend."

He took a deep breath. "Don't tell me the most stubborn woman in the country is about to balk again. I'm standing here telling you that your life is in danger and you're arguing with me. Didn't you learn anything in the spring?"

"I am not arguing."

"It sounds like it to me. How can I make you understand that these men are not your average upstanding citizens? Mad Luther would murder his dying grandmother for a ten percent cut of anything, and I suspect he wants a lot more than that. And he may want it while Sam Vitelli is burying his wife."

"The thing is…"

"Let me finish."

"You've gotten your message across. I don't trust Arthur either. There was a look in his eyes just before you clobbered him with the shovel that made me wonder if he was really worried about our safety or a part of the problem."

"You have sharp eyes. So does Sam, and you should let him handle it. I just want you out of there."

There was something he wasn't telling me. "What's going on? The Bureau wouldn't plan something at the funeral?"

"I'm no longer with the FBI, remember?"

"So you say. You didn't answer my question."

"You know I can't."

"Can't or won't?

"Both."

"Ben…"

"Are we fighting again?" He had an irritating tilt to his mouth that said my mind could be easily changed if he turned on the charm, that I was too dim-witted to resist. Handsome men can be insufferably arrogant.

I looked him straight in the eye without smiling and said, "Damned right."

His jaw hardened. The hum of the drink machine grew louder in the small space. Neither of us spoke and we were silent too long—long enough for me to wish us back in the stairwell or for words to get us over the abyss. Everything should have been so simple.

But of course it wasn't.

I broke the silence first. "Speaking of Arthur… He'll be finished by now. We need to go back."

"Promise me." He wouldn't let it go.

He was right, of course, but I hated feeling like I was deserting Sam. On the heels of guilt came a sense of anger that Isabella couldn't be buried in peace.

I nodded curtly. "I need to talk to Sam for a few minutes."

"You'll warn him he's being watched."

"I won't, but he isn't a fool. He'll know something is wrong when I abruptly check into a hotel."

"Carroll, you need to learn to…"

I set my mouth in what my grandmother calls an unbecoming line. "Don't maneuver me, Satterwhite."

"Damn it," he swore under his breath.

From kissing to cussing in less than five minutes. The kissing part had been nice, though, while it lasted.

I said, "It's time to find Arthur."

Even then he didn't move for a good ten seconds. I waited, still trying to think of a way out of the hole we had fallen into. His chin was set so hard it twitched.

I turned and walked back to the empty waiting room where Arthur was standing at checkout with all the tolerance and charm of a raging bull.

"Where the hell have you been?" he said. "And where's Dellwood? He's supposed to pay this bill."

I held up my can of Coke. "*Ellwood* is in the men's room, I think." There was no cast on his hand or even a bandage, but the swelling didn't appear to have decreased any. The checkout clerk looked over her glasses at me as if I were his wife and as fed up as she was.

I handed him the Jeep's keys. "Go wait in the car. I'll take care of the bill."

He thrust the piece of paper at me and huffed himself out of the room. I'd about had enough of high-maintenance men.

The receptionist said, "Get him to take one of the pain pills Dr. Miller gave him, and he'll be in a better humor before you know it."

"I doubt it," I said with an attempt at deadpan wit. "Perhaps all of them will do the trick."

She blinked twice, and I thought if Arthur accidentally overdosed within the foreseeable future, police would soon be pounding on my door. The thought made me smile.

Sometimes I wonder what kind of person I'm becoming.

By the time I paid the bill, Ben Satterwhite was at my elbow without a trace of emotion on his face.

In all, I had spent no more than three weeks with him—five days in March and two weeks earlier in the fall. Nineteen days at most—too short a time. He was close enough that I could feel the heat off his body, making me acutely aware that all the instincts I possessed might not be enough to guide me.

I had to set my face to keep from crying.

Chapter Nine

It was dark by the time we started back to the farm. After a silent ride, we parted company with Ben, who was parked near the barn. Arthur watched him go with a pickled expression that might have had as much to do with the two Percocet tablets he'd swallowed in the car as it did with his general nature.

"Johnny Boy, get me a scotch," Arthur said to the motionless figure sitting on the porch.

Johnny flicked a cigarette over the railing and said, "Get it yourself. The liquor cabinet is still where it's always been. I want to talk to Carroll."

I started to say something about combining pain pills with alcohol. One look at his face and I decided to save my breath. I sat down next to Johnny as Arthur slammed the door.

"His hand isn't broken," I said. "That's the good news. The bad news is that none of the women at MEDAC are ever going to be in love with him."

I expected him to laugh or at least smile. He did neither. In the still darkness, late cicadas hummed in the trees as if summer had lasted into late October. There was a rifle propped against the railing. In the dim light I had barely noticed it.

When I'd been married to Daniel, a period of time I liked to call my first life, Johnny had already been with Sam for years. He did a variety of jobs, from bodyguard to fill-in cook or chauffeur—never straying more than a short distance away from Sam when they were off the estate. During the time when Daniel fell apart, Johnny would sometimes play cards with me until he came home. Isabella thought the world of him, and her opinion had always been good enough for me. If there was going to be trouble, I wanted him on my side.

Into the quiet he said, "Sometimes I think if he calls me Johnny Boy one more time, I'll have to do us all a favor and drop him in the East River, whether Sam likes it or not." The rocker creaked as he shifted.

If he was kidding, I couldn't tell from the expression on his acne-scarred face. I played it safe and asked about Sam's injury.

"Just a flesh wound. You know Sam wouldn't go to the emergency room for anything less than a snake bite. He's all bandaged and resting, thank God." He stopped for a moment. "But this thing with Isabella…it's aged him twenty years in the last six months."

"I know. He calls me after eleven o'clock occasionally…just to talk."

"If she had a bad spell, he would sit with her through the night because they couldn't give her enough morphine to keep her from screaming. The nurses tried to convince him she wasn't hurting, but he knew better.

I sleep in the apartment over the garage, and I could hear her some nights at three or four. The last few weeks, it seemed like he hardly slept at all."

"He looks it."

"That's when Arthur moved back to the house…started taking over the office and talking about Sam being too old to run things anymore. If the boss would let me, I'd kick his uptight ass out the door in two minutes."

"What do you think, Johnny? Is he?"

An upstairs light went on, spilling yellow out onto the lawn, while he lit another cigarette, pulled the smoke deep into his lungs. "I don't know. That's the honest-to-God truth. I've been working for Sam since I was a green kid, and I don't know the answer. Maybe he should just walk away. Let Arthur have it all and see how long his butt will last with the likes of those three upstairs.

"Which leads me to why I waited to talk to you. Sam doesn't want you staying here tonight…said you'd know why. You're all booked at the Orange Inn, and he said to please not think he didn't want you, but not to let you argue either." He fumbled in his shirt pocket. "I've got the address and directions all written out for you."

"Thanks. I remember how to get there. Is it because of the men upstairs?"

The cigarette glowed red against his face. "It's best if you just do it without asking questions. That, too, is a quote from Sam."

First Stan Council, then Ben, and now Sam. The

first two I had actually promised. "It seems like I'm outnumbered." I rose and moved to lean against the railing. "Johnny, about Sam…"

"Yeah?"

"Give him a while. Let him get through the funeral first. Right now he's tired and broken, but in a month he could be back to his old self, and you'll wonder why you ever worried."

"Maybe you're right," he said. "The old fox can be full of surprises."

"All right then, I'll see you tomorrow."

The front door opened and Arthur spoke from the threshold. "Johnny, are you still sitting out here? I thought you were cooking tonight."

There was no answer from Johnny.

"We were chatting," I said. "Like old times."

Johnny got to his feet and flicked a third cigarette into the driveway. "That we were. Goodnight, Carroll." He maneuvered his wide shoulders through the doorway so that Arthur had to flatten himself against the framework to let him pass.

"Goodnight, Johnny, Arthur." I started down the stairs.

Arthur said, "You won't get it, you know."

I stopped midway. "Get what?"

"Sam's estate. I've worked hard for it. You're nothing but a former daughter-in-law—not even family. I'll make damned sure you never see a penny of it, no matter what he does with a will."

The light from the hallway flooded my face as I turned, the crystal chandelier making disco patterns with the breeze. There was no way he could have missed my immobility, the sudden flush of fury in my expression. I'd had enough of biting my tongue around Arthur.

"How strange. I never wanted the money. I never wished it or craved it or needed it, never even thought about it, in fact—until this very moment. Now I've decided that I do, that I'd like to give it away to orphans, stray dogs, strangers on the street, or invest it in Enron stock. And if Sam decides he wants to give it to me, I'll see a pompous prick like you in hell rather than let you have it."

It was as good a red flag as I'd ever waved. Ben and Stan were right to be worried about me.

I checked into the old Orange Inn around eight o'clock, so tired and hungry that I felt likely to drop if food weren't put in front of me soon. Beyond that, only bed fleas would have kept me from turning in early. Quick room service took care of my hunger, and when the phone rang around eleven, I was already in a cavernous sleep. Groggy and disoriented, I answered it, wondering where I was and if I'd overslept. The light was on in the bathroom with the door almost closed. There was just enough illumination to find the phone.

Ben Satterwhite said, "Hey. What are you doing?"

"Who is this?" As if I were likely to forget.

"How many other men call you late at night?"

"You'd be surprised. I'm sleeping, or at least trying to. Did you call with sugary words of apology?"

"No, nothing like that. I called to ask what you're wearing."

"Ragged flannel pajamas. And this isn't the phone sex line. If you're desperate, you might have better luck calling 911."

He laughed, the sound a deep rich baritone that made my toes curl. "It was worth a try. Even that image will keep me awake, wondering where the torn parts are."

"That is *soooo* tough," I said. "Before I go back to sleep, was there anything else you wanted to say?"

"You're a hard woman, Davenport. You may not recognize or appreciate the effort involved, but I'm trying to get back on your good side. What do you say? Will you meet me halfway instead of being so stubborn?"

"Try harder," I said, and hung up on him.

The phone rang again almost immediately.

"All right, all right. I'm trying harder, but you know, a reasonable man might almost think you're more trouble than you're worth."

I studied flowered wallpaper that was meant to give the room a feel of the late eighteen hundreds, a long-ago time when a woman didn't have as many options. "Where are you?"

"Same floor. Just down the hallway."

"In that case," I dropped my voice to its softest, sexiest tone, "let me tell you what I'm really wearing. Oh, but…"

"But what?" There was a note of wariness in his voice.

"It wouldn't be fair to tell you I'm not wearing anything at all because you probably wouldn't get to sleep for hours, so I'll just say, *goodnight Ben, pleasant dreams.*"

"Why, you little…"

I put the phone gently in its cradle where it didn't ring again.

Five minutes passed before there was a soft knock on the door. I crossed the room and said, "Who is it?"

A muffled voice said, "Room service with champagne for Ms. Davenport."

Much later, I thought about it and decided there wasn't a woman in the country that wouldn't have opened the door under the same set of circumstances. I knew all the rules for single women staying in hotels alone and had traveled without incident in a dozen different countries. My intuition failed me. There was nothing, not even common sense, to warn me before I unlocked the door.

It wasn't Ben or room service, but a man with a nylon stocking stretched over his face, distorting his features into grotesqueness. He slammed the door backward with a violence that knocked me against the wall, and was in the room so fast I didn't have time for more than a shocked gasp before his leather-gloved hand closed over my mouth. A hairy forearm thrust against my throat, pinning me viciously to the wall.

I struggled, making screaming sounds into the gloved hand, high-pitched noises that resonated loud in my ears. I couldn't breathe, couldn't move, and began clawing at his arm with both hands. He reeked of cigars and male sweat, pressing against me too tight—trapping me. Flecks of light began to dance in my vision.

"Listen bitch and listen good," he said in a harsh, unfamiliar voice. "Forget everything you heard, and I do mean everything. Consider this your first and only warning. You cause trouble, any trouble at all, I'm coming back with this hunting knife and gut you like a deer. You got that? Forget every single word?"

I nodded. I hadn't seen a knife, but there was no reason to think he didn't have one.

"Say it!" He released a fraction of the pressure on my throat and mouth.

I sucked in air and tried to scream, only to have him increase the force, cutting off my airflow again.

"Maybe I'll just gut you here and now. Get it over with."

My hair fell in my eyes as I shook my head in frantic motion.

"No? Then let me hear you say it. *Forget every single word.* And if you try to scream one more time, it's going to be the last sound you ever make."

I was taking in huge gasps of air. "Forget…every single word."

"Every minute of the day, I'll be watching you. You understand?"

Too quick, too eager, I nodded again.

He studied my face, the dark, intense eyes boring into mine through slits cut in the hosiery. "You need more persuading," he said, and hammered his fist into my mid-section, emptying my lungs of what little air they had left.

My first thought was that he had knifed me. I collapsed to my knees, panicked to the marrow, remembering how it had been once before, struggling to draw breath with arms wrapped around myself as if to keep the blood from spilling out. Waiting for the next blow. Waiting for the final moment.

There were many things and people I could have thought about in those last few seconds—Ben, Gran, and the baby that died that long-ago night before it was even born. None of them flashed through my consciousness the way it's supposed to happen. I felt only an awful grief that this was the end.

If I had only looked down, I would have seen that I wasn't bleeding. But I didn't.

Ben found me curled in a fetal ball on the rug with the door still open.

Chapter Ten

We buried Isabella at ten the next morning in a simple ceremony performed by a local priest named Father Justice, and otherwise attended only by Sam, Arthur, and me. Johnny stood watch at the top of the hill, while the same two workers waited respectfully on the far side of the cemetery for the moment when they could complete the job.

I'll never be good with funerals. There have been too many in my life, and I avoid them if I can. The ones that deserve a special good-bye are the ones I attend. As Arthur had so kindly pointed out, I was only the former daughter-in-law, but I grieved Isabella like she had been my own mother.

There wasn't much I remembered about the first month after Daniel's murder. I relived the gruesome murder scene and the loss of our baby in a continual spiral of waking and sleeping nightmares at a private hospital. Years later, I still have terrible dreams about that day. Not so often anymore, but vivid enough to wake me sweating and struggling when they occur.

As nervous breakdowns go, it probably wasn't an especially bad one. It seemed so at the time. The memories of being held by Isabella were powerful and deep.

In his hotel room through the dark night, I couldn't seem to explain it the right way to Ben, who wanted me to leave at daybreak and to hell with the funeral. He was angry, and I couldn't blame him. But he hadn't lived my life for thirty years before I met him. It wasn't something I cared to delegate now.

It rained sometime before dawn, forcing more leaves off the trees. The cedars were bent with moisture, and in the west, heavy, fast-moving clouds threatened another deluge.

Sam brought a framed photograph of the two of them when they were my age. Somewhere at a ship's rail, he stood behind Isabella, laughing, both arms wrapped around her on a day so perfect I could see the sunlight glinting off her chestnut hair.

At the end, Father Justice himself sang *Ave Maria* in a strong tenor voice that would have brought an audience to its feet in Central Park. When the last notes echoed across the valley, Sam kissed the photo and tucked it inside the casket before closing the lid.

By then, even Arthur had moisture in his eyes.

I didn't ask him what had become of the three men from the library. It was none of my business, nor did I want it to be. He had avoided even looking my way until we left Sam alone with Isabella for a last, private goodbye.

We were almost to the hilltop where Johnny waited. "Don't come back," Arthur said. "Stay away from Sam."

My feet froze to the path.

Funerals have a way of taking the edge off your outrage. I opened my mouth to tell him I really didn't want a dime of Sam's money, that I had spoken in anger.

Johnny heard him and said, "Some day, Arthur, I'm going to have to kill you in a very bad way."

"Don't bet on being around yourself, Johnny Boy." Without glancing at me again, Arthur walked on toward the house.

I looked back at Sam beside the casket, and out of nowhere came a little shiver of electricity, a foreboding running up between my shoulder blades. The trouble was that I had no idea who it was intended for—Sam, Johnny, or Arthur.

Perhaps even me.

"Watch out for Arthur," Johnny said. "You've made him your enemy. He won't forget it."

"It seems to be a habit of mine. I lost my temper, which isn't hard to do with him. I said something I regret, for Sam's sake if for no other reason."

He followed my gaze to where Sam was just getting to his feet. "He's in for a rude awakening."

"Sam or Arthur?"

His face twisted. "Both, I'm afraid, but I was talking about Arthur. He's seen his big chance and doesn't want to miss it."

"What do you mean?"

He studied me for a moment. "Arthur has climbed in bed with sharks. He either thinks Sam doesn't know or that he can have it both ways, counting on Sam to protect him. But he can't." He stopped and shook his head.

I waited.

"You don't want to know any of this," he said. "It's why Sam has kept you away all this time, even with Isabella dying. He'd have a fit if he thought you knew even this much, so don't worry him with it, especially now."

I held out my hand and he took it. "Promise me you'll look after him. You may be the only person left he can trust except me. And don't joke about killing Arthur, please. Sam won't like it, you deserve better, and who knows, he may not be as bad as we both think."

"He is," Johnny laughed. "The only way I can stand to have him around is to think about killing him."

"Consider this, then. If anything happens to Arthur, how many legal and not-so-legal fingers will point straight toward Sam because he's your employer?"

"OK, OK. Don't worry about it. Maybe I won't off him. Maybe I'll just truss him up like a turkey and keep him in the basement."

"Johnny…"

"Relax. I'm not ready to murder the little weasel yet. I'm just letting off steam, and I figure it won't hurt old Arthur to worry about whether he's going to wake up tomorrow morning."

I tried to look in his eyes, to read his expression, and I swear to God I couldn't decide if he was telling the truth. There were a lot of things I could have said. Like for instance, that he might want to be careful about poking sticks at skunks and snakes. I didn't. Instead, I waited for Sam and sat in the porch rockers with both of them, looking at old photos—remembering the good times with Isabella.

There was one of Daniel as a boy of about eight, even then looking willful and petulant, a look I learned to know well. Young girls know so little about character in men. What seemed like daring and strength and bravery turned out to be the worst kind of debauchery and self-indulgence. He had a cruel streak, which I later realized I hadn't recognized because none of the men in my life had possessed it. I should have gotten down on my knees and apologized to my father, Randolph, Stan—all the decent men who were around when I was growing up.

After forty-five minutes, I said my goodbyes, looking back once as I drove away. I had the same kind of feeling I got more and more often with my grandmother when we parted, the yearning to take one last look in case we never saw each other again.

It wasn't that I never wanted pages to turn in my life, but sometimes the chapters moved so swiftly it seemed like speed-reading—fast and final enough to make my chest ache with apprehension.

The drive back to the coast was uneventful, and

by five-thirty, I was in Wilmington with a whole new set of problems.

Davis worked part time with the construction company after school and was still at the Harbor Island site with Jinks, where they were fitting pickets in the upstairs deck railing. I had a sudden memory of his dreadlocks and sullen manner, marveling that overnight he had moved from one stage to the next. Not all the way, mind you, but enough that he was responsible and fun to be around again.

They looked up when they heard my footsteps.

"Oh, it's you," Jinks said. There was an iffy tone in there somewhere.

"Thanks," I said. "That's not much of a welcome for the one who writes the paychecks. You were expecting maybe Pamela Anderson?"

He ran a hand through his hair, tightening the band on the long ponytail. "More like one of the Ruggiero brothers."

Davis grinned. "Or maybe all of them."

Jinks gave him a warning frown.

"What happened?" I asked.

They had the look of raccoons caught in a flashlight beam and surrounded by trash—proud, embarrassed, and guilty as hell.

"Don't tell me the painters quit with our deadline looming," I said.

"Worse than that," Jinks said. "I fired them early this morning."

I drew a deep breath and paused for the count, which seemed to be happening more and more lately, or maybe it was just the construction business in general. "I left town at noon yesterday. It's a good thing I wasn't gone a week. Couldn't you have talked to me about it first?"

I thought it was a fair to mild statement considering it was going to take me days to find more painters and I'd have to pay a bonus to finish the job even close to on time. In reality, it was a minor setback in a business where they happened daily. With a little sleep and a throat that didn't feel as if it had encountered the Boston Strangler, everything might have been worked out as usual.

Jinks straightened. "Look, Carroll, I'm either the supervisor or I'm not. You can't undermine me by waltzing in and out of here questioning how I handle the subs. I should have fired them yesterday. Danny Ruggiero showed up drunk again this morning, trying to pick another fight. I told him to leave and come back sober or not at all."

The top of a sail drifted past, just visible over the hedge rim along Banks Channel, while images of a knock-down-drag-out fight floated through my mind.

"Then what happened?" I asked.

"What do you think? He had the neighbors coming outside by then. He was carrying on like a wild man, shouting that he would show up any damn way he pleased and if I didn't like it I could go straight to hell.

I couldn't let that happen, so I slapped him around a little."

"You didn't?"

"Of course not," he said irritably. "It was all he could do to stand up, but you can be damned sure I wanted to."

I love the construction business, but anyone who tells you men aren't as touchy as women is a damned liar. "I'm afraid to ask where the other brothers were?"

Jinks looked heavenward. "Right there beside him, hollering that if Danny couldn't work, no way, Jose, were they going to work. I'm telling you, I don't give a shit how good they are as painters. Lately, they're nothing but trouble, take twice as long as they should, and I'd had enough. I canned the lot of them, and if you don't like it, you can fire me, too, because I won't put up with their crap another day."

"Why haven't you said something before now?"

"I have. You just weren't paying attention. I was about to fire them yesterday when you interrupted, coming in here trying to turn on the girlie charm, wanting to keep everybody happy-happy."

This time I might have to count to a hundred. *Trying to turn on the girlie charm?* That part really stung. It was hard to believe he had ever been half-smitten with me.

I forced myself to take a deep breath. Good supervisors weren't hanging around in trees. I gave him my sternest look. "All right, you've got a point.

Perhaps I shouldn't have interfered. But for the record, what I saw yesterday was a full-scale testosterone brawl about to erupt. And may I add, at three-to-one odds, you were about to get your ass kicked."

Davis snorted, "Jinks can take all three Ruggiero brothers any day of the week. Don't you worry."

"Maybe, maybe not. However, I'd like to just entertain the possibility that the dock or tile men might also have waded into the fight. And then where would you have been? I'll tell you—the local jail—while I'd be looking at a big insurance increase and one or more lawsuits against the company."

With a stubborn set to his chin, Jinks wasn't looking repentant. "You might wind up in court anyway. Danny said he was gonna sue my butt, yours, and the company's."

"Great," I said. "*That's* what I wanted to hear." My mind was already switching to work mode, racing through painters' names, discarding them, and wondering if there was any way to placate the Ruggieros at this point.

Jinks unbuckled his tool belt. "I can tell by the look on your face that you're planning something. If you're thinking of hiring them back, I tell you I won't work with them again."

I sighed. "Be reasonable, Jinks."

He turned his back on me and began to gather his tools. "Time to fold the tent, Davis. Can you catch a ride home with Carroll?"

Davis looked first at Jinks, then at me. We were two of his favorite people, but I wasn't the one who spent a full year mentoring him as a friend. In a popularity contest between us, Davis was not about to step over to my side of the line. I didn't know myself what was about to happen. How could he?

A mulish expression settled over his face. "Well, hey, why don't I just hitchhike home while the two of you act like a couple of pig-headed idiots?"

It was not my finest moment. "You'll do no such thing," I snapped. "Randolph would have a fit, and you know it. Wait for me in the car. And Jinks, I suggest we go home and cool off before we say something we'll regret. I'll let you know in the morning what we'll do."

He took his time winding an orange power cord, all seventy-five feet of it, into a neat circle before tucking the ends neatly in place. "Don't bother. You haven't been listening to me for the last month or more. What you mean is that *you'll* decide what to do and how to do it, and if that dictates I have to kiss Danny's fat butt, then that's just too damned bad for me."

"That isn't what I said and you know it. Look, I've got a business to run, deadlines are looming, and I'm not sure there's even the smallest chance we'll find more good painters in a hurry. What in the double hell do you expect me to do?"

"Ah, shit," he said with disgust. "I guess I expect you'd just better get yourself a new super."

My mouth hung open while he walked away from me and got in his truck, closing the door carefully before driving away. Davis took half a dozen steps toward the disappearing truck, the sag to his shoulders telling another part of the story.

I put the tools in the garage and locked up, expecting the white Ford truck to reappear any minute so we could both apologize.

The truth was, it had been a long two days, and if sleep hadn't been such a pressing need, I might have handled things differently, but there and then I didn't want to deal with any of it. Jinks carried a cell phone the same as I did.

I was sorry we didn't use them.

A silent Davis refused to look at me all the way home. I dropped him off at Randolph's before continuing on down the drive, trying to remember when home had last looked so good. I intended to sleep with the bedroom windows open and let the fresh salt air fill my lungs with renewed vigor before one more builder turned to serious drinking.

Charlie was in a huff despite the fact that Randolph kept him supplied with fresh food, water, and so many peanuts that I threatened to put him on a diet. When I asked if he had been a good boy, he turned his tail feathers in my direction and relieved himself, making it plain what he thought.

For such a birdbrain, it's often hard to believe he doesn't know what he's doing. One yellow feather, not quite plucked, stuck out at an odd angle on his head. Together with his red irises and rapidly dilating pupils, it gave him the look of an escaped psychopath on the prowl. If I had put my finger inside the cage at that moment, he would have done his best to take it off.

"You can kiss mine, too," I said, "you scruffy little sack of feathers."

I thought morning would be time enough to make amends to all the affronted in my life.

But by the following morning Jinks was almost dead.

Chapter Eleven

The doorbell rang a little after four o'clock in the morning. I found a haggard, bleary-eyed Sam Vitelli on my front porch.

My shock must have been evident. "Sam? What are you doing here? Come in, come in."

"Forgive me for showing up in the middle of the night." His footsteps faltered over the threshold like those of a man on the verge of collapse.

"Is something wrong?"

"Yes and no," he said, sagging. "But nothing that I care to disturb you with at this hour. I wanted a place where I could lay my head down on a soft pillow and go to sleep. I knew it was unwise, but I thought of you and just started driving."

"Oh, Sam." I might have gotten choked up if I'd been awake. "You know you couldn't possibly be more welcome in my home. It's just...such a surprise."

"I dare say it is, after my policy all these years."

"Come in the kitchen," I said. "Let me make you some coffee and something to eat."

With hesitant steps, he let me settle him at the kitchen table.

"No coffee or food, though a glass of milk would be nice."

I poured the milk and watched his fingers close carefully around the glass before getting another one for myself. A striped navy tie fell out of his pocket. I picked it up and laid it across the back of his chair.

It was warm in the kitchen, and he looked ready to doze off before he reached a bed. I could think of a number of questions—like where was Johnny, for starters. In all the time I'd known Sam, Johnny had been close by. Something had happened. That much was certain.

"Here's to cows," I said, raising my glass, "and to Isabella." It was a silly, irreverent thing to say just fifteen hours after we had buried her, but it was a toast to the times she'd said, *drink your milk; you'll feel better*. He knew what I meant.

"Ah," he said, a half smile crossing his face. "Exactly."

When he had drained his glass, I said, "You aren't fooling me, you know. In the morning I want to hear the whole story of why you drove almost two hundred miles to the coast in the middle of the night. But stay, please, as long as you like. Gran will invite you to dinner and stuff you with one of Lucille's famous peach pies. We might even take you fishing. The ocean air will have you sleeping like an infant."

His eyes were almost closed already. "We'll see...we'll see. I never thought to ask if I was interrupting anything or if you had another guest."

A polite way of asking if I had a live-in?

I laughed. "Not likely." And only then wondered what I would do if Ben Satterwhite showed up.

Peggy called the next morning at a little after seven. Sam was still sleeping and I was running late, gulping strong coffee in an effort to jerk myself awake. I had fallen into bed after settling Sam in my father's old room, and my head was filled with the fuzziness that comes from pulling yourself out of a deep sleep. It took me seconds to remember who she was.

"Well, good morning, Peggy Hollowell. You're up and busy."

"It's a school day." Her voice had a jumpy, breathless quality, as if she might be jogging in place or near tears. "I haven't called too early, have I?"

"Not at all," I said, as if I'd been up for more than fifteen minutes and hadn't needed a chilly shower just to get this far. "What can I do for you?"

"I couldn't wait any longer. Did you talk to the sheriff? Please, please, please tell me you didn't give him my name."

"No," I said, "of course not. I told you I wouldn't, and I wasn't going to let a little thing like handcuffs make me change my mind."

"Oh, I never thought…?"

"I'm teasing you, sweetie. I don't go back on my

word, and most of the time Sheriff Council is a big pussycat, the same as he was when I was your age. I did talk to him. He wasn't ecstatic about the situation, but he'll go with it for now. Did Davis give you the message about the shoes?"

She let her breath out in a whoosh. "Yes, ma'am. I'll give them to him in school. He said you wouldn't tell, but I was afraid you would anyway."

A muted male voice in the background said, "Peggy, who are you talking to? I thought I told you…"

There were muffled sounds, as if she had cupped a hand over the mouthpiece. I heard her say, "No one. Just a friend about homework." More inaudible words, and then she was back on the line saying, "I've got to finish my chores. See you at school. Bye."

Charlie was begging for his morning bite of rye bagel with cream cheese, the sun was shining in a deep blue sky, and the second cup of coffee was just beginning to work its magic when the phone rang again.

A resonant male voice I didn't recognize said, "My daughter just telephoned someone at this number. Can you tell me who you are, please?"

"May I ask who's calling?" In spite of his polite request, there was a tone in his voice I didn't like. The last thing I wanted was to get Peggy into trouble with her father.

"Hollowell," he said, "Reverend Hollowell. Let me explain why I'm calling. I haven't been well, and my daughter has to help out around the house. She disobeyed me this morning by making a phone call when she should have been doing something else. I'm sure you understand the need for discipline of our teenagers and how important it is to know who they call and why."

Well, not really, I wanted to say, pegging his voice as ex-military, maybe even retired military. I stalled, figuring it was the only way to handle the situation until something intelligent popped into my head.

"You'll have to forgive me," I said. "I woke up later than I intended and my brain isn't functioning yet. You say someone phoned here?"

"My daughter, Peggy."

"Oh," I said. "Hang on a second." I reached over and knocked four times on the kitchen table before putting him on hold, thought fast, and came back with an awful lot of fluff-bunny in my voice. "Sorry about that, but there's someone at the door and my cell phone was ringing. Isn't that just the way it goes sometimes? Listen, I have to run, but it seems apparent to me that Peggy must have called my niece when I was in the shower. I have no idea why. It must have been about school or something because I'm pretty sure they're in classes together. So…I think that probably explains it. Now I've really got to answer the door. Bye."

Ninety-nine and three-quarters percent of the time, scrupulous honesty is my only policy, but I'm never brilliant in the early morning, and it was the best I could do. If it had been ten o'clock, I could have come up with plausible scenarios to satisfy a dozen controlling fathers.

Still in my robe, I went out to the end of the driveway for the newspaper. Davis was waiting for the schoolbus playing catch football with himself, pretending not to see me until I spoke from three feet away.

"Still mad at me, Davis?"

"Yeah, a little," he said without smiling. "Does it matter?"

"Yeah, a little," I said, watching him stare at the paved road, the woods across the street, the football—anything but me—which I took to mean there was nothing *little* about how mad he was. "Quite a lot, you know. Enough so that I'll try to talk with Jinks this morning, without losing my temper again, and see if I can smooth things over. You know I wouldn't want him to quit, don't you?"

"Because he's a first-class foreman?"

"That, too, but also because he's a friend and a good guy. Even your Aunt Lucille likes him."

At last a partial smile. He was probably thinking about what Lucille would do to me if she found out I'd quarreled with one of her chosen few. He didn't know the half of it.

"OK then." He tossed the football back into the air. "Better be quick, before somebody offers him more money."

"There's one more thing. Thanks for passing the message on to Peggy about the shoes. Can you do me another favor and tell her as soon as you get to school that it wasn't me she talked to this morning? It was my niece. Her dad phoned, wanting to know who she called and why."

"Wow," he said. "Way to go."

"You realize I lied to a parent. It isn't illegal, but I'm not feeling very proud of myself."

"I told you she says he's mean to her. I think it's worse since her mom died, enough so she's scared of him, anyway."

The yellow New Hanover County bus turned the corner. Several responses came to mind: that every teen thinks at least one parent is mean, that a little healthy dose of *scared* might help keep her from sneaking out to meet boys in dark and isolated places, that maybe this was the reason daddy was checking up on her.

I said, "Do you know any specifics?"

With a squeal of brakes, the bus stopped beside us. Davis shook his head. "She won't say anything to me." He climbed on the bus, and just before the doors closed, leaned out and added, "But I'll bet she'll talk to you."

Oh great. I sighed, wondering how I had gotten myself embroiled in the affairs of an age group whose every problem had the potential to become a major crisis. On the other hand, I remembered with stark clarity the way I felt after my mother died and the effect it had on my teen years. Not only had I refused to listen to anything my father or Gran tried to tell me, but the pattern became so ingrained my worst mistakes were made a long time afterward.

Peggy's mother had only been dead since last year, when she would have been fourteen—the same age I was when my mother drowned. Couple that tragedy with an overly strict father and you had a recipe for disaster.

I went back down the drive, passing Randolph's cottage. He was at his front door before I got more than ten feet past his porch.

"Hold up," he said. "Am I to understand you fired Jinks?"

I raised my eyes heavenward. "Of course not. He quit in such a fit of temper I could barely get a word in edgewise, which may or may not have been my fault. And before you say anything else, I'm on my way to bribe him to stay, if only people will have the decency to let me get some clothes on. And good morning to you, too."

He grinned and cleared his throat. "Excellent. It can't be easy working for a woman." With that, he went back inside and closed the door.

Whose side was he on, anyway? I continued on to the house, pondering the odds of putting together an all-female crew just to show the lot of them. Whoever declared women to be more emotional than men never had to deal with construction crews. I hadn't yet needed to tiptoe around a woman's ego on a job site.

Within fifteen minutes I was in the Jeep early enough to beat most of the traffic down Market Street and Military Cutoff Road. By seven-forty I was pulling into the Harbor Island job site behind a parked Wrightsville Beach fire truck and an EMS vehicle.

Chapter Twelve

The firefighter's nametag said SR Daniels, and he was at my window before I could turn the motor off.

"You'll have to move the car, ma'am. You can't block emergency vehicles."

"Of course," I said. My heart was beating faster. "What's going on? I don't see any smoke."

He pointed toward the side of the lot. "Pull over there, please."

I obeyed and made a speedy exit from the Jeep. "I'm the owner of the property. Can you tell me what happened? Is there a fire?"

"We're first response, ma'am. We answered a call about an injury and arrived just before EMS. They're with the man now. Can I have your name, please?"

"Carroll Davenport," I said over my shoulder, hurrying toward the house, where I'd spotted Jinks's white Ford pickup parked close to the attached garage. I had to blink twice to be sure. The back window was shattered, the truck bashed in along the sides as if someone had rammed it with a backhoe.

A car door slammed behind me, but I kept going until I found Jinks stretched out on the cold garage floor surrounded by the emergency medical team and another fireman.

The orange-checked shirt he was wearing when he quit had been cut off and left beneath him. He lay with swollen eyes fixed on the ceiling, an oxygen mask over half his face, and a blood pressure cuff on his right arm. From the doorway, I could hear his labored breathing.

Until a hand took me by the arm, I didn't realize the fireman was still behind me. "You'll have to step back, ma'am."

I took two steps and came up against the garage wall, but not before I caught another glimpse, this time of his chest, which seemed to be a mass of red and purple bruising.

"What happened?" I said to Daniels.

He led me out of earshot. "Can you give me his name?"

"Jinks Farmer. He's my job supervisor. What happened to him?"

"Looks like he got the hell beat—or kicked—out of him, and not recently either. From the contusions, my guess is he's got at least one cracked rib and maybe internal injuries."

It was cold in the garage, and the early morning fog had left a layer of moisture on the concrete floor.

"How bad is it? Can I talk to him?"

"It's hard to tell. I've had my training, but I'm no expert. It all depends on what the docs find in the emergency room. He's pretty much out of it, and I don't think he's going to know you, so it would be better if you followed the truck to New Hanover Regional. They'll be loading him out of here pretty quick now."

"You said not recently. What do you mean?"

"He could have been there for hours, even overnight from the look of the bruises."

"Do you know who found him?"

A voice behind me said, "I can answer that question."

"Stan. Am I glad to see you."

Daniels nodded. "Good morning, Sheriff."

"Morning, son. You mind if I talk to this little lady?"

"No, sir. I've got to get back to the station, anyway." He took a few steps before turning back. "You'll want to take a quick look in the house before you leave."

"Uh huh, I'll do that. Can you do me a favor and tell my deputy to move my vehicle? And what might I be finding inside?"

"You'll see," Daniels said, walking away. "You can't miss it."

We stood by in silence as they loaded a groaning Jinks onto the gurney and into the EMS truck. When the doors closed, I realized I'd been clenching my teeth.

"Ever had a broken rib?" Stan said, studying a four-foot section of a two-by-four in the garage corner.

I shook my head.

"Because I have. Believe me, he's not having any

fun right now, and not for a good while longer, either. Now, we might as well go inside and see what the man is talking about."

I was prepared for the worst. Even so, it was a jolt to see the word *BITCH* painted on the wall in three-foot, glossy black letters, not only in the kitchen, but in almost every room of the house. Someone had spent more than a little money on spray cans of paint. They had also used their artistic talent spraying walls, cabinets, ceilings, and doors.

"Damn it all," I said.

"Somebody must have been ticked off big time if that word is meant for you. You have any other women working on this job?"

"No. I'm the only bitch around here."

He swiped a finger across a thick swath of black and rubbed. The paint had dried enough not to stick. "Sometimes the word is used with homosexuals. Does that fit any of the crew?"

"I don't ask about their sex lives, but I doubt it. Most of them have wives, and those who don't seem to spend an awful lot of time talking about women. I haven't paid much attention, although you know how men chatter on a construction site. If one of them was homosexual, I would have heard about it."

Stan said with gravity, "The amount of damage makes it look personal to me. I want you to give me a list of everyone you've ticked off or fired in the last three to six months. I've got a feeling this was aimed straight at you, and I don't mind saying that I don't like the look of it."

"Fired? I can't remember the last time I had to fire someone. You won't believe it, but the ticked-off list won't be much longer, and there's no one on it that would do this. Even the Ruggiero brothers that Jinks fired yesterday wouldn't do anything this serious."

For a little more than six months, my life had been reasonably sane and without violence of any kind. I had no desire to start watching for boogey men around every corner again. Not now or ever.

I gave him Danny Ruggiero's phone number. "If you don't like it, how do you think it makes me feel? I thought I put all this behind me last March."

Stan took aviator sunglasses out of his pocket and put them on against the eastern brightness. "And this time you're going to do what I tell you, right?"

He had such a resolute expression that I couldn't help but smile.

"Of course," I said.

He stopped in his tracks. "I don't want to see you laughing, missy. You better sit up and listen or I'll lock you up if I have to. The next time it could be you they beat with a two-by-four."

It was a technique that no doubt worked much of the time. Lord knows, many a man in New Hanover County had straightened up and flown right after Stan gave him the *don't mess with me* speech. And if I hadn't known this huge bear of a man since I was a baby, if he hadn't patiently baited my hook hundreds of times, I might have quaked in my shoes, too. But I did respect him. That was a whole different matter.

"Yes, sir," I said with a smart salute.

He reached out and gave my hair a sharp tug, the same way he used to tweak my pigtails. "That's better. Now, come along. We're going next door to talk to Myra Winstead, and you better behave yourself."

"You know I love older ladies."

We cut across a yard filled with jelly palm, nandina, and late blooming oleander that encircled a beach cottage smaller than the surrounding homes. It was the kind of house people had the sense to build when beach houses were for kicking back instead of for show—a time when smart people built only what they weren't afraid to lose to hurricanes.

A tiny woman with what was once called a healthy tan opened the door. She wasn't a day under ninety or a pound over the same number. Early in life, Gran cautioned me against judging a book by its cover. Myra Winstead was a good example. She was wealthy enough to reside anywhere in the world, from Tokyo to Fifth Avenue. Instead, she chose to live alone in a 1950's cottage on Harbor Island, walking to the beach every morning, rain or shine, indulging a passion for gardening and giving her fortune away with great deliberation.

Since we had started the job next door, she'd been

over at least twice with home-baked cookies for the crew. For all I knew, she could have been feeding them lunch every day, because they had clammed up when I suggested they might not want to take advantage of a woman of such advancing years.

"Good morning, ma'am," Stan said. "I'm Sheriff Council, and I think you already know Ms. Davenport. You mind if we come in and ask a few questions about last night?"

"I know who you are, Sheriff." Her voice fell midway between Lauren Bacall's husky drawl and a young parakeet learning to talk. "My late husband was a big supporter of yours when you played football and an even bigger one when you ran for sheriff." She held the screen door wide. "Come in, come in, both of you. Carroll, how's your grandmother?"

"Just fine, Ms. Winstead. Like you, she'll probably live to be a hundred and ten."

"God forbid. Come on back to the kitchen. I was just going to have a cup of tea before I take my morning walk."

Stan said, "We don't want to hold you up."

"You won't. The water is hot and the cups are on the table. I had no intention of leaving anyway before I found out how that nice young boy is doing."

"He's gone to the hospital," I said, "with possible broken ribs and internal injuries."

"Oh, dear. I hate hearing that. He's such a polite, good-hearted soul. As soon as the garbage truck leaves, he rolls my trashcan back to the garage for me. He's been doing that since the first day he arrived."

I nodded. "That sounds like Jinks." I'd watched the way he treated my grandmother.

Inside, the furniture hadn't changed in fifty years. It was an interior the movie studios could film without bringing in a single prop. I was willing to bet that if I got down on my hands and knees, I could find a watermark on the pine paneling from Hurricane Hazel in 1954. She led the way down a narrow hallway with a naked twenty-five watt bulb and into a kitchen with one of those old-fashioned circular fluorescents in the center of the ceiling.

The kitchen smelled like my grandmother's where Lucille baked every day, trying to tempt her into eating more. We sat at the table in chairs so delicate I was afraid New Hanover County's sheriff would wind up on the floor. I tried hard not to laugh at the look on his face. When she produced warm scones and marmalade butter to go with the tea, all the while keeping up a steady flow of small talk about *my boys* next door, I wondered what she would say if I asked her to move in with me.

"Now," she said, sitting down. "Ask all the questions you want, Sheriff."

I had the feeling that if it took all day, she would be pleased to have the company.

"What time did you find Jinks, Ms. Winstead?" Stan asked.

"About ten after seven. I roll my trash out to the curb early on Friday mornings, you see. I heard something in your garage and went to investigate, thinking, you know, that it might be an injured animal or something. But it wasn't, was it?"

"No ma'am. Did you hear any other noises before you took the trash out?"

"Not this morning."

"What about vehicles?"

"There was nothing in the yard except the white truck, and I knew whose that was. I also know what time it came in last night, but not how it got in that awful condition. That I didn't hear at all, probably because I was watching television. One doesn't hear as well at my age, you know, and I'm afraid the volume might have been turned too high."

Stan took a sip of his tea, his thumb dwarfing the delicate cup handle. "So do you remember what time his truck got here? Last night, did you say?"

"Of course. It was about ten-thirty or maybe a little later. I went to the kitchen for a glass of water and noticed when he pulled in the drive. I assumed he just came by to check on the place like he usually does and didn't think anything about it at the time."

"No," I said. "Why would you?" *But maybe, just maybe, his scuzzbucket of a boss might have guessed.* He had never said a word to me about the extra duty.

"May I?" Stan reached across the table for another scone. "Ms. Winstead, after it got dark yesterday, did you hear anything that seemed unusual—voices, vehicles, radios, boats?"

"Voices. Not vehicles or boats—just voices. But you know how sound carries across water, especially on a cool night. If the wind is right, I can hear snatches of conversation from boats anchored way out in the channel, so last night they might not have been coming from next door at all."

Stan pulled a small notebook from his back pocket. "What time would you say this was? Before or after the white truck arrived?"

"Oh, definitely before. Perhaps fifteen, twenty minutes before. I had an extra ear out, you see, because the Joyners on the other side are down in Charleston for the week."

"But you didn't hear the truck get knocked around?"

"No," she said, a deflated expression crossing her face, making her look even older. "*That* I didn't hear. Do you think he lay there suffering all night because of me?"

Stan, who was more than three times her size, leaned his huge shoulders across the table and said gently, "Ms. Winstead, Jinks Farmer is a friend of mine, and I personally thank you for going out early this morning and having the courage to check the garage. Not everyone would have. There could have been a rabid raccoon inside, a vicious dog, or even worse, so don't be blaming yourself for something you had no control over. His mother is grateful, his boss is grateful, and Jinks will be out of the hospital in no time at all to thank you himself. Now, are we all clear on this?"

"Yes, I do believe we are." There was a tinge of pink high up on her cheeks as she smiled. "Would you like another scone, Sheriff?"

"Why, I think I would, Ms. Winstead," he said. "If my wife cooked like this, I'd be dead inside of six months and still be the happiest man in town."

Chapter Thirteen

Cutting back across the thick St. Augustine grass, I said to Stan, "Remind me to call Opal and tell her what a nice man she married. Not that crack about her cooking, of course, but how kind you are to old ladies." I elbowed him in the arm. "I'm thinking maybe you need to show that sensitive side to inmates at the county jail. Have a little tea and scones together."

He snorted. "She knows. I tell her all the time. Besides, Myra Winstead reminds me of my grandma and yours. I feel sorry for her living alone at her age, still pinching pennies. I see a lot of old people—mostly women—with their money tied up in the house, unable to keep it up and not wanting to leave."

I laughed. "You don't know, do you?"

"What? That the houses in this neighborhood are worth a lot of money? It won't do her any good unless she sells. That route leaves her sitting in a rocking chair on the front porch of a nursing home for a year or two at most."

"*This* sweet little old lady was a Franklin before she married, the only surviving heir to a steel fortune worth more than twenty million dollars."

He had the look of a man who'd had a coconut dropped on his head. "You're kidding!"

"No," I said. "Her daddy had the good sense to sell out the business long before the steel mills went downhill or moved out of the country. She's been trying to give the money away for years, but even with the stock market down, it just keeps growing and growing. The first year's interest alone would have been a million dollars or more. Imagine how much compounded interest and investments have added to it by now."

"Well, I'll be," he said, shaking his head. "People are full of the damnedest surprises."

There were now nine or ten vehicles in the small yard, including those belonging to the dock and tile men, which meant I had workmen to deal with. And there was a newer, spiffier Wrightsville Beach police car.

I said, "We've got more company."

"Uh huh." Stan snapped his fingers as if he had remembered something important, when in fact he forgot nothing. "And speaking of surprises…you're not off the hook yet, young lady."

"When exactly did I get *on* the hook?"

"When I heard your company arrived in the wee hours of the morning." He raised thick eyebrows, peering over his sunglasses, giving me an unyielding stare that I'd called the *evil eye* at fifteen. "It was well before you made that crack about tea with the inmates, which I'm not gonna forget, by the way. You want to tell me about him?"

I should have pulled my own sunglasses out and put them on. "Not especially. Are you checking up on my night visitors now, Stan? How did you hear, anyway? As if I didn't know."

"Now don't go getting on your high horse, missy. Randolph was looking out for you, as always. You think a vehicle is gonna drive onto your property, right by his bedroom window at four AM, and he won't get up to check it out?"

"It wasn't anyone you know. Just a friend. Don't worry about it."

Seconds dragged by. The dark glasses were firmly back in place, and even though I couldn't see behind them, no one would have misunderstood his take-no-prisoners expression. It must have scared the hell out of new recruits.

"Don't be trying to flim-flam me either, girl, because you know it never works. Now, I'm gonna have a word or two with Chief Hammond to make sure his boys don't miss that two-by-four in the garage. You get your crew to work anywhere but inside, and when I return, you better be ready to tell me what Sam Vitelli is doing in my county."

"How did you know?"

He grinned. "For thirty years I've been telling you I've got eyes in the back of my head. You just don't want to believe it."

I waited for the sudden, ear-splitting roar of the high-pressure water pump to cease. At least the dock men were back to setting pilings. "And besides which, I just confirmed your suspicions. Right?"

"You got it."

The tricky devil. I watched him stroll over to slap Parks Hammond on the back before shaking his hand. In all those years you'd think I'd have learned not to take the bait.

In quick order, I sent the tile men away, warned the dock guys not to enter the house or touch the truck, and made a few phone calls, one of which was to line up an electrician. The other two were to the hospital and my Nationwide agent. There was no word yet on Jinks's condition.

Payton Gray answered the phone himself. "Hang on, let me find a chair first. Whenever you call, I know it's going to cost Nationwide a bundle."

I like Payton. He's the kind of good old boy who gives G.O.B.s a good name. Mostly he's funny and had rather have a good time than make money, although he does plenty of that, too, in between hunting and offshore fishing in *The Naughty Nancy.*

In the past year, I had submitted three claims to Nationwide totaling almost a million dollars. To their credit, the insurer paid every dime. Payton had a point, but my responsibility stops at arsonists, hurricanes, and lightning strikes. At least this time nothing burned to the ground.

"Careful," I warned. "I'm a stockholder now as well as a client. Anyway, you know I call just to hear you tell me not to worry my pretty little head."

He guffawed. "OK, I'm sitting now. Fire away. Let me have the bad news."

"I need a claims adjuster at a job site, a little matter of glossy black paint on the interior walls, an assaulted foreman in the hospital, and a pickup truck which is probably totaled. There is *some* good news. The truck isn't mine."

He sighed. "Which property?"

I gave him the address for retrieving the policy number and my cell phone number so the adjuster could reach me sooner.

"Are you sure," he asked, "that there's only one property involved?"

"Come on. I can't be the worst in town."

"You are. Except for one client with six drivers under the age of twenty-five, one of whom decided to set fire to Daddy's new Porsche while it was still in the garage. Burning the whole house down because his old man wouldn't let him take the car to Myrtle Beach for the weekend seemed a little extreme to me, even for a kid only seventeen."

"There," I said. "See how lucky you are. At least I'm sane."

"Not quite how I would put it, but you lead an exciting life, I'll grant you that."

"Payton, if you had the time, I'd let you follow

me around for a week to see how dull my life really is. You'd be asleep within an hour."

"I wouldn't be brave enough. This old ticker couldn't take it."

"Dream on," I said just as my phone beeped an incoming call. "Sorry, I've got to run. Must be Hollywood checking in." I disconnected and dialed Randolph back with a sense of foreboding, the sound of Payton's big laugh still ringing in my ears.

Randolph answered on the second ring. I could tell by his voice that something was wrong.

"Where are you?" he said, quickly to the point.

"I'm on Harbor Island. What is it? Has something happened to Gran?"

"No, no, not that. You may need to come home as soon as you can. There are four men at your house raising a ruckus. When I asked them all to leave, I got nowhere, even after I threatened to call the sheriff."

"Do you know who they are? One of them is probably a houseguest."

"The old guy I saw come in late last night wouldn't tell me his name. Only other one I know is Ben Satterwhite." *Old guy* was about the same age as Randolph.

"Ben is there? Well, damn it."

"Time enough for that later. Just come on home before they start busting up the place."

"Stan is here. Do I need to bring him with me?"

He hesitated. "Not yet, I don't think. What's Stan doing…?"

I cut him off. "I'll explain later. I'm on my way."

"Meanwhile, I'll try to keep them from killing each other."

I can't always tell when Randolph is joking. Gran has known him since he was a boy and says his sense of humor is beyond dry—it's *dehydrated*.

"You're kidding, I hope."

"Only halfway, honey. Just get here. You'll see what I mean."

Stan was still talking to Chief Hammond, ambling toward the house. I interrupted them at the same time the roar of the compressor started up again. "Call me on my cell phone. I've got to rush home."

There was that eye again. He stopped in mid-sentence. You'd have thought he didn't trust me.

It wasn't as if I would ever lie to him out of disrespect, but I might not tell him everything, and he knew it. What I needed to learn was that he seemed to know anyway. I could feel his eyes on me all the way to the street.

There was little traffic as I turned west on Causeway Drive. Ordinarily I would have been home in fifteen minutes or less, but as luck would have it, the Wrightsville drawbridge was just opening. The light was red and the bars down, which the bridge tender does anytime of the day or night for commercial traffic.

Running the light was not a problem, but an Evel Knievel car vault across the open span was too exciting for me, no matter what Payton thought.

There was nothing I could do except turn the motor off and wait impatiently.

And wait, and wait.

A slow-moving barge was approaching from a quarter mile north of the bridge, in no hurry. Behind it were three tall masts, sailboats staying well back from the barge undertow, determined to make the same window of opportunity.

The day was getting warmer, and with the sun streaming in the driver's window, I was becoming uncomfortable in my long-sleeved turtleneck, feeling irritable at my poor choice of clothing until I remembered it was to cover up the bruises on my neck.

After the bridge, I caught every red light between Military Cutoff and Market Street—eight in all. I had never counted them before. My fifteen minutes was shaping up to be thirty, a result of poor planning that was beginning to have a real impact on the area. Too bad politicians don't get little juju jolts every time a driver curses them for screwing up a really nice town.

At the next light the phone rang again. Stan said, "You heading home to warn Sam Vitelli?"

"Randolph called. He seemed to think I was needed there—something about four men about to break my house apart. Where are you?"

"About ten cars behind you. I got a call from

him, too." His radio was grinding out static in the background. "You think you can fall in close behind me if we make some noise with this buggy?"

"What do you think? Who taught me how to drive?"

He laughed. "If your insurance is paid up, hang on."

In seconds he had lights and siren going and was passing me in the center turn lane. I pulled out behind him, my emergency lights flashing, and tried to keep up. We remained in the center lane as if it were I-40 built there for our own personal use, sailing through another light at seventy miles per hour.

Payton Gray should have been buckled in the passenger seat.

Once he turned onto Porters Neck Road, he cut the siren and lights, slowing down only once to fifty-five on a sharp curve. For the first time that I could remember, there was no other traffic. In minutes we were pulling up in front of my house, where the drive held four other vehicles. I recognized only Sam's rental, which had been there when I went for the newspaper earlier that morning.

Stan met me as I opened the Jeep door. "Let me have your house key. Just out of caution, I'm going in through the garage and kitchen. Randolph has got to be inside with the others or he'd be hightailing it down the drive by now. Give me one minute, then go to the door and ring the bell."

I showed him the house key and only then remembered the most important thing. "Ben Satterwhite is one of the four men. Don't shoot him if you can help it."

He grinned. "After working so hard to get him back here? Not likely."

As if I hadn't already figured that out.

Chapter Fourteen

When Stan disappeared around the corner of the garage, I unlocked the glove compartment where I've kept a gun for years, more for peace of mind than anything else. Alone on dark roads or isolated job sites, the gun was always reassuring. It also served as a harsh reminder of occasions when I'd needed one badly. This time, there was nowhere to put it except the waistband of my jeans. Frankly, I'm not the type. Feeling foolish, I put it back and walked to the front door.

There was an osprey calling from somewhere overhead, a sharp, clear break in the silence. The sound was punctuated only by a light wind rustling in the live oak leaves damaged by Hurricane Elizabeth.

I rang the bell of my own house and waited, having no idea what was going on, if anything, or what to expect.

Arthur Weiss answered the door, throwing it open with impatience. If I had been the Avon lady, he might have snarled like a pit bull. As it was, he was a little nicer than that—but not much.

"You!" he said, damnation in the single word. "You've got a lot to answer for. Get in here!"

"Arthur!" I mocked in return. "I hope you're making yourself at home."

The look he shot me would have fried an egg on a hot summer day. He turned and strode back down the hall toward the living room, tossing over his shoulder, "We're in here."

There were five men now, including Randolph, the only one relaxed enough to prop his feet on a footstool. Johnny sat on the sofa, a yard or so away from Sam, who was still dressed in pajamas and a light cotton robe that had belonged to my father. There were dark rings under eyes that seemed to have sunk back into his head. I had known all along that he was exhausted, but for the first time, began to wonder if he was ill.

Ben Satterwhite stood by the window, clean-shaven, looking tan and seriously appealing in a blue polo shirt until he returned my glance with a frown of disapproval. A casual observer might never have realized my pulse had increased just by being in the same room with him. But if he were going to act as if this situation was my fault, I might have to buy him a one-way ticket back to the islands.

I took a deep breath. "Will someone please tell me what seems to be the problem?"

Johnny and Arthur began to speak at the same time.

I cut them off. "Wait, both of you. I think I'd like to hear Sam's version first."

Arthur said, "This is none of your damned business."

Stan's evil eye would have come in handy. I made an effort at a fair imitation. "You're in my house making so much disruption that someone thought it advisable for me to come home. I'm damned well making it my business. Sam?"

"Arthur has some judicial papers, I am sorry to report, that suggest I may not be of sound mind and body."

"Suggest, hell," Johnny blurted.

"His remedy," Sam continued, "would be involuntary commitment. Needless to say, we disagree on this matter."

Of all the problems I might have expected, that would have been last on a list of hundreds. "You can't be serious. That's the most ridiculous thing I ever heard."

"The judge disagrees," Arthur said. "So do the depositions of five out of seven members of the corporate board, including Sam's own sister. All of you are standing in the way of a bona fide legal document."

Johnny got to his feet. "You sneaky little shit. I should have beaten you to a pulp years ago and stuffed your rotten carcass with concrete. Sam is saner than anyone on the board, including your own mother, and you damned well know it."

"Sit down Johnny," Sam said. "I'm not going anywhere with Arthur. You know that."

"Don't bet on it, Johnny Boy. And when that happens, you'll be out of a job and back on the streets where he found you."

"Maybe," Johnny said. "But you'll be dead."

"Johnny!" There was steel in Sam's voice. "That's enough."

"It's unlikely," I said to no one in particular, "that a court order issued in the state of New York would be enforceable in North Carolina. I also doubt a judge would issue one without Sam appearing before him."

The derision on Arthur's face told me otherwise. "Not New York. It was signed by a judge in Orange County, North Carolina, and there's nothing any of you can do about it. As a family member who cares about my uncle, I came all this way to pick him up so he wouldn't be carted away forcibly by strangers. However, that's still an option, and only requires a phone call for a private ambulance to be here in short order. Now what do you say, Sam? The easy way or the hard way? You know what will happen if you don't."

Johnny stood up. "You blood-sucking, ungrateful snake. After all he's done for you? There's only one way you're taking him out of here and that's over my dead body."

Sam laid a hand against Johnny's sleeve until he sat back down. "Arthur," he said to me in an unsteady voice, "thinks we don't know the plan was to drug the two of us, Johnny and me, at dinner yesterday. We would both have been hauled away, no doubt. One little thing went wrong. Someone was kind enough to slide a note under my door telling me not to drink the wine. We left in separate cars with Johnny as the decoy. Otherwise, I would have been hidden away in a private hospital by this time."

"That's enough," Arthur said. "You see what I mean?

He's been fixated on the subject for the last six months, acting deranged, imagining plots, hiding money, keeping important business decisions from the corporate officers. I'm the chief financial officer, for God's sake."

"What about Frank?" Johnny said. "Frank Foppiano was dead in the garage a little before midnight. I saw him myself."

"That's a fucking lie." Arthur raised his voice. "Foppiano flew back to New York early. He left for the airport right after dinner."

I didn't have a clue which of the men from the library Frank Foppiano had been. Sadly, I wasn't sure I cared. But I did care about Sam, who was looking paler by the minute.

Satterwhite hadn't moved from his position across the room. He was propped against the east wall, his arms crossed over his chest. If he had been standing beside me, I might have found the nerve to slap Arthur senseless. Instead, he shook his head in disgust and threw me another disapproving look, as clear as if he had said out loud, "Now do you see what kind of people these are?"

I turned my attention back to the villain in this piece. "What did you mean, Arthur, when you said, '*You know what will happen if you don't*'?"

"Why don't you ask Sam," Arthur said. "Ask him if Isabella died of natural causes or whether she was hustled along. I suspect he was planning it for a long time and it unhinged him. My God, people. Do you think we didn't pray long and hard about whether Sam would live more than six months in prison? Believe me, a hospital is the only way. No one need ever know, and with a few months of treatment, he'll be back to his old self."

I was having real problems visualizing Arthur at prayer. Sam's eyes were squeezed tight as if he were shutting something out. I wasn't buying the idea that he hustled Isabella's death, but who knows what any of us would do under the same set of circumstances? His reply might not be something I wanted to hear.

"So you're blackmailing him," I said.

"Not at all. I'm offering him a way out, and strongly advising him to take it."

"Sam?" I said.

He opened his eyes. I saw the same haunted look, but something else, too, something of the former Sam—a look of outrage. "I do not know whether to laugh at him or do his mother a kindness and have Johnny shoot him, because he will be dead soon anyway. Arthur has crawled into bed with a nest of crocodiles who are using him to get rid of me. Afterward, they will eat him alive. He thinks they may let him keep control of the financial side, that my home, the money, the power can all belong to him. Instead, he will have my sister, God help her duplicitous soul, weeping over his coffin. And do you want to hear the amusing part?"

So far he hadn't looked at Arthur.

"Please," I said.

"Long before Isabella died, I decided I had had enough. What good was the money? Daniel was dead; Isabella was dying fast. There was nothing left to enjoy. I was working out an agreement with certain individuals so that Arthur could keep himself in Italian suits and expensive cars that he never drives faster than sixty miles an hour.

"He must need me alive in a hospital somewhere, at least for a while, or it would have been me on the garage floor instead of Frank. What he wants is a quiet coup that won't upset my friends, including you, who were to assume my derangement because he was building up a case ahead of time.

"So, you see, all his trouble was for naught. As it turns out, I was way ahead of him, though for different reasons. The money Arthur so desperately craves is safely where he cannot get at it—ever—even with the finest legal assistance. The same goes for the real estate, especially where Isabella is buried."

At last he turned his gaze in Arthur's direction. "And as for Isabella..." He paused. "I gave her my offer, my pledge, not once but nightly, to end her suffering. I would have done so without hesitation. She did not want it. And if I find that someone—anyone— shortened her life by even an hour, only God will be able to protect him." He settled his head back against the cushion, his eyes still locked on Arthur's.

No one moved in the room.

With heightened senses, I could smell the candle

wax from the mantelpiece, the ashes in the fireplace grate. The hair on the back of my neck was tingling. Arthur was like a man in shock. Had he really believed Sam was so old he could be out-maneuvered?

The silence lingered another few seconds. Time enough for me to wonder again what in hell was taking Stan so long.

I said, "The ball has landed in your court, Arthur. Not only is he not going with you willingly, there are five of us here to back him. This would be a good time for you to leave my house, don't you think? Give it up. Your plan won't work."

He blinked several times in rapid succession, moving out of a trance and straight to fury. Gone was the civilized veneer. No more Mr. Nice Guy.

"So I move straight to Plan B. Did you idiots think I was so stupid I wouldn't have a fucking backup plan?"

Plan B was a silver automatic pulled from his jacket pocket, very similar to the one I'd just put back in my glove compartment.

I thought it was, without doubt, a good time for Stan to make an appearance.

As if in slow motion, I saw Satterwhite moving away from the wall, Randolph and Johnny scrambling to their feet, Sam's head snapping up in surprise. The gun was aimed straight at my heart.

"Stop!" Arthur said. "Right there—the three of you. Now get over against the wall together." They unfroze themselves and did as they were told, moving in a clump to where Satterwhite had originally been standing.

"Now, Johnny. Put your gun on the floor and slide it over here. Careful. Sam values her life more than his own."

I held my breath, knowing how much Johnny hated him, guessing at the amount of willpower it would take not to shoot.

"Johnny…" Arthur warned.

He put the gun on the Oriental and kicked it so hard it slid off the rug and went clattering across the kitchen tiles. I watched it come to rest against the pantry baseboard.

"Now, stand up," Arthur said to Sam.

"Leave him alone," I said. "Can't you see he's near to having a heart attack?"

"So much the better. Simpler all around if you just go ahead and die, old man. Get up. We're walking out the front door with Carroll as insurance. If you resist in any way, I'll have to kill her, which I may do anyway if I find you put everything in her name."

Sam was too clever for that, I thought. I hoped.

Sam got slowly to his feet, and somehow Arthur began herding us toward the front hallway. I cast a fast glance over my shoulder and felt a surge of sorrow that Randolph would have to be the one to break the news to my grandmother. I thought there was something important written in Ben's face beyond his condemning scowl, but I couldn't tell what it was.

I blinked and turned around. Sam took my arm, seeming to straighten a little as we moved toward the front door.

"Go," Arthur said, "before I change my mind and kill you both here and now."

"I might have something to say about that," Stan said in a deafening voice. "Don't move a whisker, son. Now, drop the gun or you'll be the dead one here."

Chapter Fifteen

Nine out of ten people seeing Stan Council looming over them with a gun—all six-feet-eight inches and three hundred pounds of him—would do as they were told. Even Arthur was smart enough to obey, especially after Stan clamped a hand as big as an anvil around his wrist. The gun slid out of limp fingers onto the hall rug.

"Who in the hell…?" Arthur started.

"Your worst nightmare," Stan said, "at least until some high-priced, uptown lawyer gets here. Ben, you want the pleasure of cuffing this overdressed asshole, seeing as how he interrupted your vacation and all?"

"If I can keep from strangling him." Ben crossed the room. "What took you so long, anyway? Vitelli, you OK? Carroll?"

"Now I am, but Sam needs to sit down. Johnny, can you help him back into the living room?"

Between us, we got Sam in the same chair while the others dealt with Arthur, finally cuffing him to a straight-backed chair with his hands pulled behind his back.

Randolph was leaning over Sam. "What's wrong with him? He's white as a sheet."

"He needs a doctor," I said, noting the increased pallor and rapid breathing that seemed to have escalated steadily during the whole episode.

Sam shook his head. "No doctor. There is nothing wrong with me that a week of sleep will not cure."

"Johnny, what do you think?"

"I vote yes. Boss, we're overruling you."

Sam shook his head for the third time.

"You're clammy," I said.

Stan walked over and got down on his haunches at Sam's level. "Mr. Vitelli, we talked once back in the spring, and it seemed to me you were a sensible man. I know you just buried your wife and for that I'm sorrier than I can say, but you need to listen to these people. It looks to me like a heart attack about to happen. You're pale, sweating, breathing too fast—all classic symptoms. Now how about it? What's it gonna cost you to get checked out?"

"My life, if Arthur has his way. Let me rest a few minutes longer while I think about it."

Stan studied him for several seconds longer. "All right, but if I think you're getting worse, there won't be an opinion poll. You look to me like you're having pain anywhere in your body, and you plain and simple don't get a choice. Understand what I'm saying?"

"I do, but I will be all right."

Stan grunted in my direction. "Keep an eye on him while I deal with Mr. Pussytoes."

Arthur was staring at Satterwhite, a sneer on his face. "I'm not saying a word to some hick town sheriff without a lawyer present. I insist on making a phone call as soon as possible."

Stan walked around his chair slowly, hands on his hips. "Aren't you moving a little too fast? Have I read you Miranda? Or booked you at the county jail?"

Arthur had to crane his head back to look up at Stan. He said peevishly, "I know my rights."

"Do you, by God?" Stan stopped in front of him. "Was it your right to come barging in here threatening Mr. Vitelli? Was it your right not to leave when you were asked? And was it your right to wave a gun around and force two people to go with you? Let me tell you something. You ought to be thanking me for intervening instead of giving me a hard time. You know why? If you had taken one step over that threshold with these people at gunpoint, I wouldn't have had to file kidnapping charges against you. Someone would have been giving me a medal for killing you."

"Unless, of course, I beat you to it," Ben said.

Stan shrugged. "Either way, you'd have been deader than a duck in hunting season." He began circling Arthur, close enough to knock his chair over if he brushed against him. "If this had been just between you and your uncle, I might not have minded so much, being as you're both from New York and all, but then you had to pull a gun and threaten a lady.

We don't much cotton to that kind of behavior around these parts."

"A lady!" Arthur sneered. "You think? Is that why she couldn't wait to shack up with a common gravedigger? Or whatever he is? If you ask me, he's got small-time lawman written all over him. Did you know about this, Sam?"

A muscle jumped along the side of Satterwhite's face. He never looked my way, but both hands curled into fists. I thought it might be rather enjoyable if someone took a swing at Arthur, since there seemed to be no tar and feathers handy.

Sam waved a dismissive hand, leaving me in the dark as to whether he knew about Ben's background.

Stan stopped behind Arthur and said in a voice that would have frozen a snake in mid-strike, "Is that right? Well, good for her. But son, you need to be real careful here. I've known this pretty little girl since she was born, was good friends with her daddy. You better be watching your attitude, your mouth, and your dumb-assed behavior. Otherwise, someone might have to take you out to the alligator farm and teach you some manners. That someone might have to beat you to a bloody pulp and then watch what them big old boys do when they smell you. You get my drift?"

This was supposed to help Sam recover? It could guarantee a heart attack. Stan was laying it on thick, like an uneducated, redneck sheriff. I almost believed it myself, even though I'd never heard of an alligator farm north of the South Carolina line. Arthur didn't know better, though, and was fast losing his arrogance. For that I would tolerate the *pretty little girl* reference, as if we were still living in the fifties.

I could hear the creak of Stan's gun belt each time he shifted. I didn't interrupt. No one did. It occurred to me that Johnny should have been the happiest one among us, given that Arthur was getting his comeuppance. Instead, he was huddled over Sam, talking in low tones.

I caught Stan's eye, raising my brows and nodding my head toward the kitchen.

He said to Satterwhite, "Can you watch this sorry excuse for a relative for me while I get a glass of water?"

"Glad to, Stan. Take your time. Maybe he'll try to run and I'll get my chance to whack him once or twice."

Stan reached into Arthur's jacket and pulled out the court order. "I'll just take this piece of paper with me and read it over. Check on those signatures and all. Light's better in the kitchen."

"I'll show you," I said.

I turned on the water in the kitchen sink and led Stan out to the garage where we couldn't be heard. "You can't let him go until we find a place to hide Sam, and he needs to see a doctor first. The sooner the better."

"What makes you think I'll let the son of a bitch go?"

"I know you. When you start posturing and bluffing like a redneck jerk, it means you're up to something."

"Which ought to be locking his sorry butt up, or at least making him pay through the nose for a lawyer to spring him. Sometimes you're too smart for your own good, missy. You know that?"

"I know," I said modestly. "How long can you stall?"

"What did you have in mind?"

I told him what I was thinking. He made some creative additions, and we stopped at the kitchen sink before returning.

Once back in the living room, Stan continued the noisy tirade about pathetic relatives in general and ill-mannered boys from other parts in particular. "I sure am sorry. I don't know how it happened, but your court document fell in a sink full of water. Didn't even get to read it before the ink got smeared, signatures and all. Ain't it a shame." He crammed the dripping paper into Arthur's pocket.

He failed to mention that modern inks are tougher than we think and that it was possible someone had to use a plastic scouring pad.

I went to check on Sam. "How's he doing?"

"I don't know," Johnny said. "Maybe his breathing's a little better, maybe it isn't. I still think he needs to be checked."

"Do not fuss, Johnny," Sam murmured. "You are worse than an old-maid aunt."

"Listen," I whispered. "Both of you. We have a plan. Just act surprised and play along, no matter what I say.

"Johnny," I raised my voice and Stan stopped in mid-sentence. "I don't care what he wants. He's caused enough trouble and I want him out of my house. You understand? Sam, you shouldn't have come here in the first place, and God only knows what kind of scum might follow Arthur down here next. I'll show you how to get to New Hanover Regional. After that you're on your own. Now go get his clothes. I want you both out of here in five minutes flat."

They were appropriately startled, enough to fool Arthur, I hoped. If not, I'd have to develop an alternative plan, and the only Plan B that came to my mind was to drop Arthur down a deep hole. Stan would never go for that one, though, and I was too squeamish.

"She's right," Sam said to Johnny. "I should not be here. My clothes are down the hall, last room on the right. Go on and get them."

Randolph said, "Carroll, what are you…?"

"Stay out of this, Randolph."

"But you can't…"

I ignored him. "I don't want you back here, Sam. Ever. You understand? My home can't be used as a hideout. Not by you or anyone else."

"Yes," Sam said. "I understand."

Johnny was back with clothes over one arm.

I said, "Don't bother to get dressed. For all I know, Arthur has friends on their way to help him right now. Let's just get you in Johnny's car and go."

Across the room, Stan stood in front of Arthur and winked at me. "Seems kind of harsh to throw an old man out on the street."

I tried for an angry tone. "Stay out of it, Stan. This is my house. You just make sure this over-educated prig is gone when I get back, and I don't much care how you do it. You think the two of you can handle him? Because Randolph is going with me."

Randolph said, "What's gotten into you? I'll not be a party to this. The man is ill. Can't you see that?"

I put my hands on my hips. "Help Johnny and don't argue with me. My mind is made up."

So was Randolph's. I could tell by the fire in his eyes that he was going to have plenty to say about everything as soon as he got the chance. I'd be lucky to get to the car before he started.

"Don't hurry," Stan called as we opened the front door.

I couldn't resist. "We won't. And please don't get blood all over the good rug." Not a nice thing to say, but at least we could make Arthur sweat a while longer.

Ben's eyes followed me out the door. I could feel them burning the back of my neck. If he didn't like it, he could go home to Maine and annoy some other woman. And good riddance. I didn't turn around.

Chapter Sixteen

The hardest part was mollifying Randolph, who seemed to think I had lost all semblance of both common sense and manners. He wasn't far off. I could have found a gentler way to get us out of there, but with no time to plan, the words had poured out of their own accord. Some of them were closer to the mark than necessary.

Randolph sometimes forgets that I've passed the *thirty* milestone and haven't been a teenager for a long time. He's inclined to view any questionable decision on my part as a personal affront to his influence, the same way he did in my rebellious youth. Granted he had good reason back then. If it was forbidden, I wanted to try it—everything from ignoring curfews to hitchhiking and high-speed racing. The worst decision of all was marrying Daniel Vitelli despite Randolph's wise counsel. I think he still sees worrying about my judgment as part of the natural order of things.

He calmed down as soon as I told him Stan had approved the plan.

There were two rental cars to deal with, so I drove one and Randolph the other, with Johnny and Sam following in the Jeep. It wasn't far, only about a mile to the Cornelia Nixon Davis Health Care Center down Porters Neck Road. Not so very long ago it was called a nursing home, and the front porch was still lined with rockers and wheelchairs, which held people in various stages of alertness.

I led them around back, parked, and got out of the rental. Johnny lowered his window. "Wait here. I'll be as fast as I can."

Sam said, "Here?" No one over seventy wants to get near a nursing home. There was a look of shock on his face.

"Trust me," I said.

At my grandmother's instigation, we had both given sizable chunks of money to the Center. She said half her friends were here and it was where she'd wind up, too, if she lived long enough. I couldn't argue with that. When the day came, it would be her choice to make—my house, hers, or where her friends were. It didn't seem all that complicated to either of us.

Jackie Martin was at her desk behind a door labeled *Director* when I put my head in. She was a medical doctor specializing in geriatrics, maybe forty-five and rounded, with coal black hair beginning to show gray and eyes that crinkled when she smiled, which was often. The staff and residents adored her.

"Have you got a minute for an urgent problem?" I asked.

"Of course. Come on in." She closed the file she

was working on and moved it aside. "Is your grandmother with you?"

"Not this time. And, Jackie, the problem is a doozie."

She laughed. "There hasn't been one in weeks that wasn't. Fire away."

"Don't say no, please, until I finish. If you agree, there'll be a large check in the mail."

"Another one?" She smiled before putting on a serious face. "Carroll, we'll take the money and be glad of it, you know we will, as long as you aren't bribing me to do something illegal or unethical, but my decision has to be based on what's good for the Center. Now, having said all that, why don't you just explain the situation."

"You can hide someone for me…someone whose cunning relatives and corporate board want him committed to a mental hospital by any means possible, fair or foul, when he's as sane as you or I. His wife just died, and he's ill both in body and spirit. I'll pay whatever it takes, but I want him hidden away, under a different name, where they can't find him. It might be days or it might be weeks, just until he gets some fight back in his system. He may be ill, but I promise you, there is nothing wrong with his mind."

She studied me for long seconds, tucked a strand of dark hair behind one pearl-studded ear. "I have a few questions. First, are there existing court documents involved?"

"Not legible ones, no."

"Please don't tell me what that means. Secondly, how long ago did his wife die? It isn't all that unusual, you know, for the surviving spouse to have a temporary breakdown."

"We buried Isabella yesterday. She died three days ago." Tears suddenly welled in my eyes and ran down my cheeks.

I didn't see it coming. Sometimes I surprise even myself.

Jackie passed me a box of tissues and waited patiently. There must have been hundreds of others who had cried in the same chair.

"Do I have time to think about this, maybe discuss it with a couple of our board members?"

"No," I said. "He's in the car."

She took a deep breath. "Well then, I have one last question. What name do you want to use for his admission?"

"Oh," I said, my mind blank, tears beginning to flow again.

Jackie said, "I get the distinct impression this is very important to you."

I laughed with relief, ending on an obvious hiccup. "You have no idea *how* important—maybe even a matter of life or death. I'll never be able to thank you enough, but I promise to try."

"Good," she said, picking up a pair of half glasses. "Now dry your eyes, think of a name, and let's go find this fabulous patient."

We took an aide with a wheelchair out to the cars where Randolph and Johnny were pacing. Jackie opened the passenger door and removed a stethoscope from around her neck. "Good morning. I'm Dr. Martin. You can call me Jackie. And you are…?"

"Sam…"

"Monroe," I said. "Sam Monroe." Well, he was *almost* family.

"Mr. Monroe, your friend here has very effective powers of persuasion, so it looks as if you're going to be our guest for a while."

"Not long, I hope."

"You're the boss," Jackie said. "Most people don't want to stay long at our rates, but before you talk about leaving, we need to get you admitted. May I listen to your heart before we put you in a chair—just as a formality of course?" She didn't wait for his reply, but pulled off the stethoscope and listened carefully to his chest and back.

After taking his pulse, she asked, "Are you on any medications, Mr. Monroe?"

"Just Hytrin."

"For high blood pressure or prostate problems?"

He seemed embarrassed. "My blood pressure is fine."

"That's good. And how long since you've had a full night's sleep?"

Sam shook his head. "I cannot remember."

"Weeks," Johnny said. "He hasn't gotten a decent

night's sleep in weeks. Hi, I'm Johnny Rinaldi, Sam's…"

"Assistant," I interrupted, ignoring his surprise. After I'd worked so hard to get him in, I couldn't risk a change of heart because Sam had a bodyguard. And why hadn't I thought to have Johnny use another name?

Jackie straightened and said, "I think we're ready to take him in now. Mr. Monroe, do you need some help getting in the chair?"

"Just Johnny's arm, please. I am a little dizzy." The move was accomplished under his own steam, but he sat down heavily as if it had been an effort.

I gave Jackie a spontaneous hug. "Thank you from all of us. I know he's in good hands."

"You're welcome. Go away now and come back this evening after we run some tests." She patted my hand as if I were the worrying mother and Sam a young child.

I watched her wheel him away with a lump in my throat. "Hold on a second, Johnny." When the rest were out of earshot, I said, "Be sure he doesn't use his credit card, make phone calls, send e-mail, or let anyone know where he is. The same goes for you, unless you trust Arthur more than I do." I handed him a slip of paper with an address and phone number. "Use this as an address for both of you. We'll go turn in the rental cars and get you another one under Randolph's name. Does that cover most things?"

He grinned. "Yeah. Except how we're going to keep Sam here once he starts feeling better."

"One day at a time, Johnny. You just keep thinking positively and make sure Jackie checks his heart."

"And finds out whether Arthur was slipping him some kind of drug."

"Really?" I turned back.

"Once or twice I suspected it, but Sam didn't want to admit Arthur could do such a thing. Maybe now he'll be ready to listen."

"The son of a bitch," I said.

With Randolph's help, I returned both cars to Hertz at Wilmington International and rented an off-white Grand Marquis V-8 from Budget in Randolph's name. I sent him in alone for this one, thinking that if anyone should ask, a clerk was certain to remember a youngish blonde with an African American gentleman in his seventies.

Stan phoned as we turned onto Blue Clay Road. "We escorted the weasel out of New Hanover County with a western warning. If he comes back here or if anything threatens you or anyone close to you, including Sam or Johnny, kidnapping charges will be filed automatically. I probably can't make that one stick, but we'll at least get him for assault with a deadly weapon."

"How do we know he won't turn around and come right back?"

"I can't give you the details, honey, but the Bureau is on his tail along I-40. After Arthur gets on the plane in Raleigh, I'll get a phone call letting me know about it. I'll get one faster than that if he turns around. Ben has a lot of friends in the Bureau."

"Tell me why you didn't charge him anyway. I don't understand how you could let him go, and I'm damned sure not happy about it."

"Hold on a minute, honey."

He was on the road somewhere. I could hear him talking over the hum of the vehicle. "Ben says to tell you it's a little matter of professional cooperation between investigating agencies, and that you don't need to know any more than that. There are bigger fish to catch than Arthur, but he's swimming in the same pool. That's all the information you're going to get, and even that you have to keep to yourself. You understand me?"

"Keep my mouth shut?"

"You got it. That means, Sam, Johnny, Randolph, and anybody else you run across. Now, do you want to talk to Ben? He's right here beside me."

I thought of the disapproving looks Ben kept sending across the room as if everything had been my fault.

"Carroll? You still there?"

"No, I don't want to speak to Ben. Thanks, Stan. Let me know when Arthur gets on the plane. I'll feel better."

He chuckled. "I'll have Ben do the calling."

"You do that."

When we had disconnected, I filled Randolph in on some, but not all of the information. He knew me well enough to realize I was withholding something important.

He shook his head. "When did you get to be so devious? You used to be the sweetest little girl in town, and now I never know from one week to the next what kind of trouble you'll get in. Last year we went for months with nothing dangerous happening, and now look at us."

I laughed. "Must be the men in my life."

"Men aren't your problem. Trouble follows you like a tail follows a comet, like an anteater follows ants, like…"

"Stop. You can't believe this is my doing? I thought I was getting through life the best way possible—working hard, treating people well. If you accuse me of inviting Arthurs into my life, I'll move to Australia or somewhere. Then you'll never get that grove of banana trees you want to plant."

"You take chances. It's hard on the rest of us to watch, especially the ones getting on in years."

"Holdovers," I said, "from a time in my life when I was young and stupid and really did make poor decisions. See, I even admit it. But I couldn't turn Sam away in the small hours of the morning; surely you can see that. It was obvious at the funeral that something was wrong, but I thought it was just the stress of Isabella finally dying."

"The wisest choice would have been not to go in the first place."

"Randolph…"

"Hush up a minute. I'm just telling you how it looks to the people who care about you. Since when have I not told you the truth?"

"Look at it another way. Would you go to a funeral for my grandmother, or me, or Davis? Can you envision anything that would keep you away? And a better point: If I were male instead of female, would we be having this conversation in the first place?"

"This has nothing to do with women's lib."

I made a left turn onto Gordon Road and slowed for the residential area. "Think about it; that's all I ask. And think about how much I loved Isabella…how good she was to me."

Through all the years I'd known him, Randolph seldom backed down when he wanted to make a point. "Loving Isabella almost got you killed. You think no one noticed the bruises on your neck? Even with Ben down the hall, you could have wound up dead."

"He had no business telling you. Mr. Satterwhite has a lot to answer for."

"Two eyes are all it takes to notice. And for your information, he didn't say a word until I threatened to take his head off for being the cause. Then he was damned near as mad as I was."

"You thought Ben…?" I glanced sideways at his set face. "That must have been an interesting confrontation."

"I apologized. Had to. If I'd been twenty years younger, I might not have gotten out of the room alive."

The light turned green. "Sounds as if you might be living on the edge yourself, Randolph. I've been around an angry Ben several times, and it isn't an experience I'm eager to repeat."

"Then I'd advise you to watch yourself, my girl, because he's right on the brink with you. You're treating that boy like dirt. And with that, I'm going to shut up and change the subject. Tell me what Jinks had to say this morning. He did show up for work, didn't he?"

I almost ran off the road smacking myself in the head. "Heaven help me. I can't believe I forgot to tell you about Jinks." I pulled off the road into Pinehurst Pottery's parking lot where giant jack-o'-lantern bags were lined up in a row.

I took a deep breath. "He did come back, but late last night, not this morning. I think he went back to check that everything was locked up properly. The gardening neighbor found him early this morning. Someone else showed up last night, too, and vandalized the house. Whoever it was also beat Jinks badly, enough to send him to the hospital with possible cracked ribs and internal injuries."

"Jinks? And you forgot to tell me?"

He was indignant and I didn't blame him, not after everything that Jinks had done to help turn Davis around. Sometimes a fifteen-year-old will bond more readily with a stranger than his own family, and Jinks had been with the company only a couple of weeks when Davis came to live with Randolph full time. Davis had just spent a night in jail after being caught with gang members in a stolen car, and we were at a loss as to what to do. A lot of people went to bat for Davis, but Jinks was due most of the credit for being his friend and mentoring him in the building trade.

"I know. I'm sorry. There's just too much going on."

"Did you say Myra Winstead found him?"

I always forget the serious plant people around town know each other. It was her palms and bananas that got Randolph started on his tropical kick.

I pulled a phone book from under the seat. "She called 911 about ten after seven this morning. EMS was there when I arrived a little after seven-thirty. One of the dispatchers at headquarters alerted Stan when he saw who owned the property, which is why he was there when you first called me."

I punched in the number for patient information at New Hanover Regional Medical Center, gave the name Jinks Farmer, and while waiting, tried to fill Randolph in on the other details. After five minutes or more, I was informed that Mr. Farmer was still in the emergency room and that there was no information as yet. Would I please call back later?

My watch said it was eleven-thirty, and I was suddenly so hungry I could have eaten a full-size Whopper without giving fat grams a second thought.

"First things first," I said. "Let's get the car back to Johnny and check on Sam. Jackie will still be running tests, unless she thinks he needs a cardiac unit. Either way, I should be able to go see Jinks. Want to tag along?"

I pulled back onto Market Street heading north, unsure of whether it was a good thing that Jinks was still in the emergency room.

"Yeah, I think I will. That'll make your grandma and Lucille feel better, not to mention Davis, because you know he isn't going to be speaking to you for quite a while after this."

"It wasn't my fault Jinks got into such a snit."

He put on his shades, a hint of a smile lurking. "Maybe you just think it wasn't. I wisely plan to reserve judgment until I've heard the official male version from Jinks."

"Why, you cheeky, disloyal, old dog," I said. "It's for sure you aren't getting those banana trees, and I'm tempted to stop signing your paychecks just to teach you a lesson."

Out of the corner of my eye, I caught a flash of teeth as white as those of a man half his age. He didn't look worried.

"You couldn't do without me," he said.

Which was true, and had been since I was a baby. In addition, my grandmother and Lucille would be all over me, as they would say, *like ducks on a June bug.*

Chapter Seventeen

Sam was having blood drawn. Johnny waited outside the lab, propped against the wall with his ankles crossed, reading the Wilmington *Morning Star*. The hallway was brightly decorated with cheery Norman Rockwell drawings as a reminder of better times. It was warmer than a normal hospital, and Johnny looked hot and uncomfortable in his sports jacket.

He looked up sharply at the sound of our footsteps, and it occurred to me that if he reacted the same way with each passing nurse, doctor, or resident, it wouldn't take long for someone to figure out his bodyguard status.

I was more than glad to see he was staying alert, so I didn't bother telling him about the law against concealed weapons. If he had worn the gun on his hip, wild-west style, he would have been well within North Carolina law, even though it might not have been the best thing for the elderly residents' peace of mind. On the other hand, it might have added another level of excitement after Bingo and Scrabble.

Sam was just inside the lab, reclining with a frown in the kind of chair the Red Cross once used for blood donations until budget cuts pushed them to plastic.

"How's it going?" I said in a low voice.

"Slow," Johnny said. "Not much happening."

"But better than dealing with Arthur?"

"Shit, yes."

Randolph handed him a set of keys. "We brought you a present—a whitish Mercury Grand Marquis parked about five spaces down from where we were. Papers are in the glove compartment. You get caught for speeding, call Sheriff Council. You have a wreck and my insurance is going through the roof because the car's in my name and you aren't listed as a driver. So, treat it like a baby, and if you have an accident, swear I'm your brother."

Johnny grinned.

"The styling won't get any wolf whistles," I said, "but it won't be as noticeable as a luxury car, either. By the way, I should have asked earlier how the two of you are fixed for cash."

He reached in his pocket and pulled out a folded wad of bills that belonged in Las Vegas instead of a nursing home. "Sam gave me his, so we should be OK for a while without resorting to plastic."

"Don't even think about credit cards or checks, and if you need more cash, let me get it for you. Now, what about a place to stay? I'll find you a motel room as soon as we know for sure that Sam doesn't need to go to the hospital."

He shook his head. "It's all arranged. Jackie is bunking me in with him."

"Well," I said, "good for her."

"Maybe not so good for me," Johnny said, his eyes following a pair of shapely legs down the hall. "He snores like a herd of elephants."

As soon as the vampires were finished with their requisite bloodletting, Sam was whisked off for a chest X-ray and we went to find Jackie, waiting outside until she finished with a female resident using a walker who looked to be a hundred and ten. Randolph grew bored and wandered off to check the moisture level in the potted plants. He had a thing about dying flora in commercial buildings.

Jackie beckoned me in and closed the office door. "So far, we can't find a problem except for the rapid heartbeat. We're doing bloodwork now, so we may know more soon. Barring any big surprises, he won't need to be hospitalized."

"Thank you. That's a great relief. I had visions of him in full cardiac arrest." And, indeed, I could feel the tension easing in my neck muscles.

"Not on my watch, I hope. But sit down a minute. Let's talk about Mr. Rinaldi."

I sat. "What about Johnny?"

"Well, for one thing, he tells me he suspects a relative might have been drugging the patient. Said that a couple of times Mr. Monroe didn't seem to be aware of where he was. This could be true or it might mean any one of a number of other things. Do you have any information that might add to this scenario?"

"I can't say whether he was being drugged, but it would be consistent with the situation and one or more of the relatives I mentioned earlier. What kind of other things?"

Jackie studied me. "You realize I'm telling you far more than I should, but he could have been taking sleeping pills, for instance, or painkillers he doesn't want to tell us about."

"Not likely," I said. "Not with his wife dying in the next room. He was consumed with fear that she might pass away in pain or breathe her last breath when he wasn't by her side."

She nodded. "You know him better than we do. But it's also possible he could be in the early stages of some kind of dementia. Or, as Mr. Monroe says, he may simply be suffering from exhaustion. It isn't all that uncommon for one of the partners to collapse after not allowing themselves that luxury for a long time."

"Johnny would have known if he were taking something else."

"People, old and young, can be extremely clever at hiding drug use."

I smiled. "You don't know Johnny. He's been with Sam a very long time. If he suspected drugs, the first thing he would have done was a thorough search, and I do mean thorough."

She raised her eyebrows. "Speaking of Mr. Rinaldi…"

"Yes?"

"What kind of assistant would he be?"

"What do you mean?" I looked over her head at a painting of Monet's water lilies. Anyone who had taken the most basic psychology course wouldn't have been fooled for a second.

Jackie seemed amused. "Is he the typing kind, the fetch and carry kind, the sexual kind, or…?" She left the question hanging.

"The other kind," I said.

She sighed and steepled her fingers, peering at me over the half glasses. "Can you expound a bit on that? Because I take my job seriously, too, and I need to know if the shoulder holster and the bulge under his jacket mean what I think."

I was tempted to ask what she *thought* they might mean, but she was in no mood for levity, and who could blame her.

"He's a bodyguard," I said, exhaling.

"Thank you. That wasn't so hard, now was it? And since I assume he isn't law enforcement, I have to ask you if Mr. Rinaldi is reliable. Not a hothead, for instance."

"No, not exactly a hothead." I picked up a brass paperweight and put it down again.

Her voice was stiff. "Then, *what* exactly?"

"I'm trying to give you truthful answers, Jackie.

He won't run up and down the halls waving a gun, shooting up the place, but…"

"I'm very glad to hear the first part of that sentence. But…?"

"His job is to take care of Sam, to whom he's dedicated almost to a fault. He'll do whatever is necessary, even if it costs him. I can assure you that both these men would still be visiting and resting in my own home if a little matter of involuntary commitment hadn't come up."

This was the right time to reassure her by suggesting she talk to Stan, but in truth, I wasn't sure of what he might say.

She was quiet so long I expected the four of us to be thrown out, willy-nilly, into the street. "I'm reminding myself of your potential contribution, which would save me weeks of work. I do loathe fundraising."

"Do I need to increase the figure?"

She smiled. "My dear, I wasn't blackmailing you. I was thinking that I have a son in med school at Johns Hopkins and that I would sorely hate to lose this job. More than that, I could never forgive myself if something happened to one of our residents."

She stood up. "Let's leave things as they are for a while longer, shall we, before I decide whether Mr. Monroe will need to be one of them. Fair enough?"

"Yes," I said, relief flooding over me. "More than fair enough."

"Well, then. We're putting Mr. Monroe in an end room near an exit, for our safety as much as his. The exits can't be opened from the outside and our security guards check repeatedly through the night. If a door is opened, there's a silent alarm that alerts them, since we can't have our residents wandering away in the dark."

I held out my hand. "Thank you for arranging for Johnny to stay with him and for everything you're doing."

"You're very welcome. As long as you understand that I have to put the residents first. With luck, we'll get through this without incident, and I must say that so far my nurses seem to be in the most danger."

"From Sam?" I was genuinely shocked.

"From your Mr. Rinaldi."

"No," I said. "Johnny is as harmless as a lamb."

"Harmless?" She rolled her eyes. "I think not."

She laughed and walked me out to the central area where we separated, with her heading off to the labs while I went to find that paragon of sexual appeal. Clearly, I would have to view him with different eyes.

I found Johnny waiting outside yet another room, this time reading a magazine with his usual lack of impatience.

I sat down beside him with a knowing grin. "I understand you have the nurses all atwitter."

"Who told you that? Jackie?"

So it was Jackie, now? My mind refused a scenario

where he was putting the moves on the staff, including the director. What an unlikely combination.

"Dr. Martin did. I thought you'd like to know I just assured her you weren't a sex maniac, homosexual, or gun-toting hothead, so don't make a liar out of me, Johnny."

"Hey," he said. "I haven't left Sam's side for a single minute. How can I get into trouble? But thanks for telling her I'm straight."

I told him about Stan's phone call and Arthur's escort service to the county line, explaining Stan's threat of a kidnapping charge, and that Arthur was also being followed to the airport in Raleigh. I was careful not to mention anything about the Bureau's involvement.

"Is that your boyfriend's doing?"

Hadn't I just promised, less than an hour before, to keep my mouth shut? "Stan's I think, but I don't really know. What makes you think it's Ben's doing?"

"Because I asked Sam about him."

"What did he say?"

"That he'd known about Satterwhite for six months or more, and not to worry about him."

"He knew all along?"

Johnny grinned. "And more about him than you do, probably. Sam doesn't do anything halfway. Arthur was right about him, but he got the branch of the law wrong. Your man practically has FBI written on his shirt pocket."

"It doesn't bother you, does it? Or Sam?"

"Hell no. Not as long as he doesn't start barking at my door or going after Sam. Then we might have words, if you know what I mean."

"He retired in August, and I didn't expect him to show up in Hillsborough. He was worried about me, and he tends to get a little overprotective at times. I'm in a weird spot here. Will you help me make sure Sam understands that I would never be a part of spying on him?"

"Give yourself a break, kid. Sam knows how the world works, and he's not going to stop caring about you because of one former FBI agent. As long as he's good to you, that is. If not, he'll have to deal with the both of us. You tell him that for me, OK? And tell him also that he'd better watch out or he's going to have some competition."

"I'll tell him," I said, "but it looks to me like you're going to have your hands full with Jackie."

Chapter Eighteen

Randolph and I drove downtown toward New Hanover Regional. It was a clear fall day. The air seemed cleaner and images sharper. A visitor from New Mexico or Arizona would have thought forty-five percent humidity was high, but it was rare for us when the weather was in the seventies.

Jinks had been moved upstairs to Intensive Care. We stopped by the nurse's station first, where one of them recognized Randolph from his hospital stay in March for a head wound. He spent a week recovering from an encounter with a worthless character with the apt nickname of *Dog*, who also murdered my cousin, Eddie. A lot of people slept better after Dog Fowler met a suitable fate at the bottom of the Cape Fear River, especially me.

Since we weren't family, it took a combination of guile and charm to find out Jinks had been operated on for a ruptured spleen. He also had a cracked rib and a broken tibia, and as if that weren't enough for him to deal with, the doctors were also worried about retina damage in his left eye.

We found him drugged and bandaged, but breathing better than earlier in the day. His eyes were swollen almost shut, and he was hooked up to several machines, which made whirring, clicking noises that echoed like bats in a tunnel. A nurse young enough to make me feel ancient was fiddling with buttons and dials.

Randolph whistled under his breath. "Man, oh man. He's going to be one miserable son-of-a-gun when the painkillers wear off. He looks like somebody beat him with a baseball bat."

"Or a two-by-four," I said, "plus boots and God knows what else. Whatever was handy."

We were only allowed to stay a few minutes, and as far as I could tell, Jinks never knew we were there. I walked out of the room with an edgy, angry feeling, thinking that if the Ruggiero brothers had done this, I would make sure they never got another painting job in all of North Carolina. If a stiff jail sentence came out of it, so much the better.

"Don't let Davis come by for a day or two," I said. "He'll think Jinks is dying." Which he might have been if Myra Winstead hadn't heard *animal noises*.

Randolph put a hand on my shoulder. "How about we go down to the cafeteria and eat something. We'll both feel better."

We found the room crowded, but still managed to get a table near the back wall. Randolph ate fried chicken with gusto, as if the idea of Jinks being unable to eat had somehow made him ravenous. I picked at a salad plate, feeling as if Myra's orange scone was still sitting in a lump at the bottom of my throat. I'd been starving earlier, but after seeing Jinks, I couldn't seem to swallow the papery lettuce.

We'd been seated ten minutes or so when Ben Satterwhite paused in the entrance, scanning the room before heading our way. Maybe nurses fanned themselves in the same way when Johnny Rinaldi walked by, but I doubted it. Sometimes I felt the same way myself, like it was enough just to watch Ben walk across a room, manly and self-assured, the way men were before petulant and pretty became fashionable. But this was usually right before he turned critical, so there were also days when I didn't even think he was good-looking. From the expression on his face, this was probably going to be one of them.

On my right, Randolph nudged me in the side with his elbow, giving me a wicked grin.

I sighed, feeling my heart rate increase whether I wanted it to or not. "Behave yourself," I said.

He shook his head. "Girl, I swear I don't know what I'm going to do with you." Whereupon he moved to the other side of the table so that Ben could sit beside me.

"What are you doing here?" I said, staring straight ahead.

"Stan is upstairs talking to the doctor about Jinks. The nurse told us where you'd gone, and I thought I'd better come down here and check on my..." He stopped.

"Your what?" I kept my voice neutral.

"I was going to say 'my interests'. Maybe I should find a better phrase."

"Yes, you should," I said, feeling the heat from his body. "Perhaps 'ticked-off bitch' would fit the bill after you kept glowering across the room this morning as if it were all my fault."

Under the table, someone kicked me in the leg.

"Randolph, weren't you going to get dessert or something?"

"Nope. I wouldn't miss this for all the pie in North Carolina."

"Actually," Ben said, "I thought I'd catch a ride back with the two of you, since I'll be hanging out at your place for a few days."

At last I turned, startled to find his face inches from mine. "Really? And when was that decided?"

"Stan and I talked it over."

And made the decision for me. I took a sip of iced tea, tried for a bland, conversational tone. "Don't even think about it."

For a change, it was his turn to take a philosophical breath, clear his throat. "It's all settled. I'll be sleeping in the guest room."

"What amazing powers of deduction," I said with as blank an expression as I could muster. "You damned well will, if I let you in the house at all. Why would I subject myself to your judgmental lectures when you don't know me well enough to understand my present relationships, much less my past ones? How dare you be critical, especially when none of this is your business?"

He hiked his chair two inches closer. "I made it mine when *you* became my business."

I'm almost never at a loss for words and this moment was no exception. "Well, we can fix that problem."

"Dessert seems to be calling me after all." Randolph rose from the table and made a fast getaway.

Ben's breath was close enough to ripple the hair along the side of my temple. "You are the most…" He inhaled and began again. "Stan said you were mad. I didn't believe him."

"This is not a good place to have a fight."

"Where, then? And what is it with you and Vitelli? It can't be the money."

I got up from the table and began walking away. After four or five steps, I turned back, leaned close to him, and said in a low voice, "One thing you need to know, Ben. If I ever feel half as much for you as I do for Sam Vitelli, you can count yourself a very lucky man, and you'll damned sure recognize when I'm pissed at you."

I walked off with a deep pit where my stomach usually was, found Randolph, and told him I'd be upstairs.

"Ah, Carroll," he said. "What are you doing?"

There was more bite to my words than I intended, at least where Randolph was concerned. "Don't start. You can't fix this for me. Please don't try."

Upstairs, I tracked down Stan, who hadn't found

out much more than we had and was about to leave. Questioning Jinks, he said, wasn't going to happen for at least twenty-four hours.

"Has Satterwhite got a ride with you?"

"If he comes along quietly," I said. "It's up to him."

"He can't say I didn't warn him you were steamed. Does he believe me now?"

He must have seen the answer in my face because he put an arm around my shoulders, which was a bit like a sledgehammer's weight, but felt good all the same. "Do you mind if I give you some advice?"

"Why not? Everyone else is doing it today. Why should you be any different?"

"Go easy on him. I don't think he quite understands what your life has been like, even though I've told him you had good reasons for becoming a prickly little hedgehog. I'm betting he's never known a woman like you. He's a good man. Don't mess up."

"I won't be controlled, Stan."

"Oh, hell, honey. Every man has to feel like he's in control some of the time. Otherwise he doesn't feel like a man."

This time he patted me on the head, and while I was a bit old for such a show of affection, it brought back enough memories to put a lump in my throat. In simpler, long-ago days, it was a gesture signifying unstinting adult warmth, which cured almost every childhood crisis from tantrums to bad report cards.

"Talk to him," he said. "Cut him some slack. That's

all you need to do. Besides, it'll be awkward if you don't, seeing as how he's gonna be sort of watching out for you a while."

I closed my eyes, a sense of déjà vu descending. "Not again."

Stan's laugh was loud enough that one of the nurses frowned and put a finger across her lips.

"You'd better get on out of here. And don't worry. I won't murder him in his sleep."

"It isn't Ben I'm worried about."

I know when Stan is kidding and when he isn't. He wasn't smiling. "All right. I'll do my best."

"Just use common sense. That's all I ask. We still don't have the foggiest who attacked Jinks or why, so don't be going back to the job site alone or after dark. And if you see Ms. Winstead, tell her I said to keep her doors locked."

The elevator opened, depositing Randolph and Ben. Stan raised a hand and said, "Hold that for me, would you boys?"

"Wait a minute. Did you find the paint cans?"

"Not a sign of them, and the Wrightsville police have checked every dumpster on the island. I was counting on some fingerprints. You think Arthur had something to do with this?"

"No, I'm thinking Ruggiero brothers. Arthur had no way of knowing Sam was going to leave in the middle of the night, and what would be the point in beating Jinks? There's always the possibility the vandalism started as a Halloween prank and got out of hand when he showed up."

Stan shook his head. "Like I said, it looked real personal to me. Way too personal."

He glanced at Ben and gave one definitive nod before clapping Randolph on the back, getting on the elevator just as the doors were closing.

I faced the two remaining brave souls. "Just to set the record straight, in case you were thinking I'm some kind of prima donna, I do appreciate you—both of you."

There, that wasn't so hard.

They exchanged such pained looks that I knew I'd been the topic of their conversation after I stalked out of the cafeteria. It was worse than that. If I was reading them right, they had reached some kind of agreement.

Truly, I needed to spend more time with women.

I handed Ben the Jeep keys. "Before we go back, I have to run by the beach jobs. After that, I'm giving up and going fishing."

I pulled the phone directory out and left a few messages for possible paint crews while Randolph directed Ben to Wrightsville Beach. We made a loop, starting at the lower end of the island on South Lumina, where I had razed a beachfront contemporary from the sixties after several hurricanes in a row took their toll. Half the pilings were in place and the job was progressing smoothly, no more than a few days behind schedule.

At the north end of the island, the men were at the framing stage, renovating and enlarging an ugly toad into a princely, six-bedroom home due to be finished in April. At both jobs, the crews were subcontractors who didn't need or want constant supervision at this stage. Long before Jinks was back on the job, though, I would have my hands so full, I'd be wondering why I'd ever thought the construction business was rewarding.

Harbor Island was the last stop. We found the dock crew wet and muddy, almost finished with the pilings, and ready to start bolting the joists by Monday.

I was startled to realize it was Friday. My watch said it was a few minutes past two o'clock, and in another hour and a half, every construction and landscape crew on the island would be paid and leaving early for the weekend. All my own subs were being paid at predetermined stages of the job, except for Jinks, of course, and Davis, who was only part time. In less than a month, I'd be tearing my hair out with computer work, time sheets, paychecks, and assorted problems out the wazoo.

The yellow tape was missing from the garage and entranceway, which meant crime scene work was finished. All the damage on the white pickup appeared to be on the outside, so I did a quick check of the glove compartment and under the seats for valuables. Finding none, I phoned to have it towed to a body repair shop I used near Castle Hayne.

By the time I was finished, only Ben was waiting at the Jeep.

"I'm ready," I said. "Where's Randolph?"

"Off to see the woman next door."

"If he and Myra Winstead start talking horticulture, we might never get away," I groaned.

"Come on," Ben said. "Show me what happened inside while we're waiting."

I inhaled deeply, reluctant to go back in. "It's disturbing. I can do without the images until Monday. With luck and the offer of a big bonus, I'll have painters here by then."

"You're saying you don't want to see it again?"

"Not particularly."

"Humor me. I want to see what Stan thought was bad enough to spook you."

"Stan's words, not mine. I've seen worse. Come on, let's get it over with."

If everything had been smooth between us, I could have told him the black paint reminded me of Daniel Vitelli's blood all over our bedroom walls. But as things stood, there wasn't much to make me discuss my late husband's murder with him, and I darned sure wasn't in the mood for more criticism.

We went through the garage, past flies buzzing around the dried blood where Jinks lay for hours in the cold night. Ben saw it, too, and glanced at my face.

I said, "Alone in the dark, it must have occurred to Jinks more than once that he was going to die before anyone found him."

Somehow it seemed colder in the house than it had earlier in the morning, although I knew it wasn't. I shivered.

Ben made the circuit, room by room, his face grim. I was grateful he seemed to be fresh out of critical comments. In the last bedroom, he said, "The enamel paint is so thick in places they'll have to sand it down and use a coat or two of primer before the final color."

"I know what needs to be done, Ben." I kept my voice neutral, one step away from polite bordering on pleasant.

The sun had moved to the other side of the house, and Myra's trees now blocked much of the light that had poured through the windows earlier in the day.

He stopped in front of me, his eyes unreadable in the dim room. "I'm making conversation here, despite the fact that you turn into an icicle every time I get within three feet. So, I'm starting again. You have a nice touch with the crews. I expected something else."

Surprised, I said, "Like what?"

"Oh, I don't know. That you were playing at it, I guess. It's a hell of a job for a woman."

"Playing?"

"Wait, I'm screwing up. What I mean to say is

that it's a job you're obviously good at, whether you need to work or not. I should have seen it before."

"We were busy," I said straight-faced. "We had other things on our minds."

He laughed and reached out a hand to touch the side of my face. "As I remember it, there was damned little mind work involved."

He hooked the fingers of his left hand around the back of my neck and pulled me a fraction of an inch closer. His breath was on my face, the scent of his skin intoxicating.

"Ben…"

"Shhh," he said. "There isn't anything more important than this." He pulled me so close I thought my bones were melting, and kissed me like a man who'd just escaped drowning, his hands hot on my back.

I lost track not only of the time, but also the week and month. Black walls could have been flowered wallpaper as far as I was concerned, and I wouldn't have cared if we'd been in the middle of Times Square. He was good; I'll give him that.

I was saved only by Randolph's heavy footsteps on the stairs, his voice bellowing, "Are we going fishing or not?"

"Almost finished," Ben called out, and straightened my sweater with a self-satisfied grin I wanted to slap off his face.

Danny Ruggiero was waiting when we walked

outside, his van blocking the Jeep. There was no sign of the other brothers. He was dressed in baggy jeans and a red golf shirt, which couldn't hide his beer gut. On the whole, he didn't look like the kind of man who, drunk or sober, could have gotten in the first blow with Jinks—much less have put him in the hospital.

Looks can be deceiving. I had learned that much, anyway.

"What do you want, Danny?" I asked.

"I'm looking for Jinks."

"He isn't here." I could smell alcohol on his breath, but he didn't appear to be intoxicated.

"There's his truck. He must be around here somewhere."

"Like I said, he isn't here today. Now, I'd like you to leave the property, please."

He looked me up and down, glancing at Ben and Randolph standing a little behind me. "I'm not leaving until I get what's coming to us. You owe us sixty-five hundred dollars."

I blinked. "Jinks fired you for being drunk and disorderly on the job. Since you were being paid in stages and the last payment was a week ago, I can't see how you come up with that much. If you send me an itemization for the work this week, I'll go over it with Jinks and mail you a check."

His face reddened. "You're going to stiff me for all our hard work?"

"Did I say that? I intend to be fair, but not until I

see the itemized figures and have a chance to discuss them with Jinks."

"You cold-hearted bitch," he said. "That ponytail pervert will make sure we don't get a dime owed us, and you damned know it. We should have beat his pretty face to a pulp when we had the chance. I'll bring you your figures, and when I do, you better have a check in your pocket or you're going to be one sorry broad."

"Are you threatening me, Danny?"

"In front of witnesses? Hell, no. But I'm telling you we'll be coming to see you, and maybe it will be when you don't have muscle around to protect you."

Was this how it started with Jinks?

"Here's what you'll do," I said, thinking that if he wanted cold-hearted bitch, he could have it. "You'll send me the figures by certified mail and I'll reply the same way, because I've never short-changed a sub yet. Anything else on your part, such as trying to deliver them in person by stepping one foot on any property belonging to me, will get you arrested for threatening bodily harm."

"The hell you say."

"Are we clear on this?"

Ben and Randolph moved to stand on either side of me.

"Shit, no!"

"I think we are. Now get off this property and don't come back."

"You goddamned dyke. You haven't seen the last of me, not by a long shot. No broad talks to me…"

"Ben," I said. "May I borrow your cell phone?"

He took a step forward. "Sure, but don't you want me to beat the crap out of him first?"

"What about it, Danny?"

He threw a last malevolent glare at the three of us before getting back in the van, his tires throwing sand and mud as he pulled out of the yard.

Randolph shook his head. "Girl, I swear, you don't know a thing about handling men."

"So people keep telling me." I looked at both of them. "And if you make a single joke about the *dyke* accusation, you'll be walking home."

Chapter Nineteen

Never take a cell phone when you go fishing. It defeats the whole purpose if the idea is to get away and relax. I should have known better.

Sam was deep in an exhausted sleep when we checked on him, so at least for the time being, there was nothing more we could do at the nursing home.

"Go," Johnny said. "Quit worrying so much."

The equipment and bait were in the boat, and the weather was perfect for the fall run of bluefish. Given that the day had been filled with vandalism and violence, the work schedule shot to hell, and my sex life devoid of any kind of action except heavy petting, things were actually looking better.

Blades of grass in the marsh were turning gold in the clear light. There was only one other boat in sight as we made our way toward the north end of Figure Eight Island.

We got as far as Rich Inlet and anchored in twenty feet of water before the cell phone rang. When it did, Peggy Hollowell was hysterical. *Kevin? Kevin had disappeared?* So much had happened since the two murders that at first I couldn't remember who he was. And then I did—Peggy's cowardly midnight friend.

"Slow down, slow down," I said. "What do you mean, he's disappeared?"

Her voice was full of panic. "He didn't come to school again today. His mother says he went out to catch the schoolbus yesterday morning, but the driver swears he never picked him up. Something has happened to him. I know it. I just know it."

"Hold on a minute," I said. "Catch your breath, Peggy. You mean no one has seen him since yesterday morning?"

"That's what she said. They fight all the time, so she wasn't worried until he didn't come home last night. Now she thinks he ran away, and I'm not sure she cares that much."

She began to whimper, while at the same time attempting to explain to me how Kevin had no money and hadn't taken his car. "He loved that car. He wouldn't leave without it. He couldn't!"

Oh, yes, he could have, I thought. I knew because I had done it myself, not once but twice, hitchhiking to Myrtle Beach on my first such expedition, and to Daytona on the second. Exactly why I went was a mystery now, but it was all part of the anger and defiance of my unsettled youth. I could remember the feelings.

"Peggy, I want you to listen to me. Take a deep breath and calm down. Please. I'm having a hard time understanding you."

"I'm trying, but I'm just so scared. I don't know what to do."

"Try to concentrate. Let's think about it for a moment." Her breathing slowed enough that she no longer sounded as if she was hyperventilating. "That's good. Keep breathing deeply." There was a noise like she was blowing her nose, and then silence from her end.

"Are you still there, sweetheart?"

"Yes," she said in a voice that reminded me of Tully, my niece who had just turned five.

"Dry your eyes now, and help me go over a few things. You know I'll do anything I can, and so will Davis. Let's start with Kevin's friends. Perhaps they have some idea where he is. Have you contacted any of them?"

"Just Michael and Trevor, his best buddies. They haven't heard a word from him either."

"Do they know about Monday night?"

"Yes!" She began to cry again, weeping softly into the phone. "If they tell…" There was a long pause, interspersed with muffled whimpers, and then, "If my dad finds out…"

"Under the circumstances, Kevin's life could be in danger and yours, too. Don't you think it might be time to have a long talk with him?"

She squealed in my ear so loud I had to hold the phone away. "No, you don't understand…!"

It occurred to me, ungenerously I'll admit, that one might need a degree in psychology to survive the experience of raising a teenager. If I had been anything like Peggy, and I had been except for the timidity, it was a miracle my father and Gran hadn't just put a pillow over my head one night.

"Then make me understand," I said.

"He's been sick. I can't tell him."

"Is there anyone else you can talk to? I really want to help you, Peggy."

She began crying again. "I can't, I can't."

Seconds went by before it dawned on me that I was holding a dead phone to my ear. She had hung up on me.

My options were much more limited than they'd been a few days ago when I'd promised Peggy to keep her secret. I couldn't do it any longer. Chances were good that Kevin, whose last name I didn't even know, would turn up soon. He might be sullen or glad, but he'd be home, and despite what Peggy thought, his mother would be relieved. The possibility that Kevin had disappeared of anything other than his own free will was too terrible to contemplate. It would mean I was at fault for not giving Stan their names in the first place. It would mean that Peggy might also be in danger.

The empty sand flats at the north end of the island glowed in the late afternoon light as the boat rocked cradle-like in the falling tide. There wasn't a more peaceful place on the face of the earth.

What had I done?

Ben and Randolph were staring at me as I punched in Stan's cell phone number. I didn't know what they thought. I didn't care.

"Sheriff," he barked, just as I lost count of the rings.

"It's Carroll. Do you remember those two…"

"I can't talk now. I'll get back to you."

"This could be urgent, Stan."

"Carroll," he said on a long breath, as if he'd had enough of me and everything else for one day. "We're right in the middle of something you don't want to know about. Is Satterwhite with you?"

My eyes seemed to close of their own accord with the most awful forewarning. I could barely get the question out. The scent of roses was overpowering. "Where are you?"

"None of your business, missy. You know this isn't a secure line. I'll call you back when I can."

"Don't hang up, please. Just tell me if you're at the Arboretum."

There was the briefest moment of silence. He spoke to someone else and came back to me. "What the hell is going on?"

"There's a missing male teenager—one of the two kids making out in the Japanese garden the night of the murders. If you aren't at the Arboretum, just tell me and I'll get off your phone."

"Shit," he said. "Goddamn it!"

"Stan?"

With reluctance he said, "Yeah, I'm here."

"Can you smell roses?"

"I should be able to," he said. "I'm standing in the fucking rose garden. What's going on, Carroll?"

"He's sixteen years old. Is it him?"

He seemed to sigh. "I don't have a way of knowing yet. We're still digging him out."

A sharp gust of wind blew off the Atlantic. "Will you send a deputy to check on the other one? Her name is Peggy Hollowell. She lives in the white two-story house behind the bog garden."

"Hollowell," he said. "I know that name."

"The father is a minister. Church of the Faithful or Missionary Faithful. Something like that."

"Mother died a year or so ago? That the one?"

"Yes. Be careful with her. I'm not qualified to judge, but she seems to be right on the edge."

"Better the edge than dead. We're on it, missy. I'll call you."

"Wait, Stan. The boy's name is Kevin. I don't have a last name, but Peggy or Davis can tell you."

"Kevin," he said. "Hell, knowing his name makes it even worse. And somebody didn't care enough to file a missing person report."

Chapter Twenty

Randolph had the anchor hauled and the tackle put away before I disconnected the cell phone.

"We have to go back," I said, giving them a brief version of my conversation with Stan.

Over the noise of the motor, it was impossible to talk, and I waited until we were at the dock to fill them in on the details. Urgency made my words spill out clipped and rapid.

Randolph said, "Go ahead without me. I'll finish up here."

I hopped out as soon as the boat hit the floating dock. "There's no reason the two of you shouldn't keep fishing. Stan will be questioning Peggy and it will help if I'm there. She trusts me."

"I'll tag along for the ride," Ben said. "Maybe look at the roses or something."

"No need," I said over my shoulder. "This doesn't involve Arthur, and won't take long—no more than an hour and a half."

He gave me one of those impossible-to-read looks and shrugged. I didn't make a fuss. A woman has to choose her battles. He must have approved, because midway up the ramp he crooked an elbow around my neck and placed a quick, hard kiss on my mouth.

I backed away against the railing. "What was that for?"

"For Randolph. He's been eyeing us for the last hour, wondering if you're going to claw my face. Also because you're learning not to argue."

"Randolph has good reason to wonder. I could be planning to smother you in your bed tonight. If I simpered and wore a low-cut dress, you wouldn't have a clue until it was too late."

There was an ironic tilt to his smile. "It might be best if you don't talk about bed and look at me that way at the same time."

"You," I said sternly, "need to get one thing straight. There will be no bed until I say so, and that won't be until I'm satisfied you aren't a chauvinist pig in sheep's clothing. Now, I can only concentrate on one problem at a time, and today there are so many you're at the bottom of the list. If you think otherwise, you may need another place to stay tonight. Do I make myself clear, Mr. Satterwhite?"

He blew his breath out with a grin. "Clear as a glass."

It was like talking to a tabby wall two feet thick. He hooked the arm back around my neck. "What are we waiting for? I thought you were in a hurry."

My feet were planted to the pier decking. I stood

my ground. "Don't just ignore what I'm saying."

"You are more trouble than all my other women put together."

"And that would be how many exactly?"

"Only one at the moment, but don't get overconfident."

The front of the Arboretum parking lot was filled with cars, many of which were city and county vehicles. Yellow police tape blocked the entrance to the old gatehouse and extended in both directions, cutting off the main part of the gardens. At the northeast corner of the rose garden, there was a tight cluster of uniforms just beyond the lattice fence.

The courtyard fountain had been turned off, and a hushed assembly of employees, volunteers, and community service workers watched from the flagstone wall. Apart from the others stood a college student named Robert who had been working off court-ordered service hours for a month or two.

He jumped when we stopped beside him. "Hey, you're Carroll, right? I helped you mulch a bunch of flowers last week."

"What's happening?"

"There's a body in there. Either that or some weirdo buried fake body parts for a Halloween trick."

"You saw it?"

"Yeah. The rose curator had a busted underground

pipe at the faucet. She sent me to dig it up, and I found this...thing. It sure as hell looked like a real arm with a hand attached. Sheriff told me to hang around and wait for somebody to talk to me. I don't mean to sound like a jerk or anything, but I hope they hurry up because I've got a class in forty-five minutes."

We waited a few more minutes before Stan spotted us outside the taped area. He wore his grim face. I'd seen that look before. He hates it when bad things happen to kids.

I asked, "Are you able to tell whether it's a sixteen-year-old boy?"

He moved us closer to the main building, out of earshot. "At this point, all we know is that it appears to be a young Caucasian, but even that could change. There's a lot of mud. They're having to dig him out slowly to preserve any evidence."

"What about Peggy Hollowell? Was she home?"

"For all the good it's doing us. Maybe you can calm her down. We're not getting much out of her except a whole lot of tears at this stage." He pointed toward the far side of the pond. "Go with her, Ben. Make sure she stays on the sidewalk and in one place. I'll be there in a minute."

We dipped under the police tape, walked through the gatehouse, and past the corner of the rose garden fence. Seventy-five feet farther around the curve of the pond, we found Peggy sitting under a Japanese maple with a female police officer. Her head was resting on crossed arms in her lap, and as we got closer, I could see her shoulders moving.

Under the tree and around her feet, miniature maple leaves made thin patches on the ground, still retaining tinges of green mixed with gold. Behind her, blue water lilies lingered in the pond.

"Let me talk to her alone," I said to Ben. After passing me a large white handkerchief, he stood far enough away so he wouldn't spook her.

"Peggy?"

She raised her head a few inches. "Carroll," she said, and fairly flew off the bench into my arms in a storm of weeping.

"It's all my fault," she said between sobs. "If I hadn't sneaked out with Kevin, none of this would have happened. And I should have told somebody… God, I am so scared. He's going to kill me, too. I know it."

"The sheriff won't let that happen," I assured her, and then felt like weeping myself, because I couldn't be certain. "Come on now, sweetie, let's get your eyes dry so we can figure out what to do."

"She wanted you to have these." The female officer handed me a large brown grocery bag neatly folded over and fastened with an oversized X-shaped paperclip.

"What's this?" I said.

"My shoes," Peggy sniffled. "You asked for our shoes, remember? Mine and Kevin's? I never had a chance to tell him yesterday, but I guess you won't be needing them now." Great tears began to roll down her cheeks again. "I wish I hadn't..."

"Stop," I said gently, the way a real mother might. If this was as close as I was going to get to motherhood, I might as well do it right. "The person to blame here is me. I should have given the sheriff both your names right away. I was wrong not to."

She looked at me with naïve innocence. "But you promised."

"Yes, I did. And I remembered that promise instead of using my good judgment as an adult. It was a stupid thing to do, and I won't ever forgive myself."

"I trusted you," she said. "If you hadn't given me your solemn oath, I wouldn't have told you anything."

Out of the mouths of babes. Bless her. I took a deep breath and let it out slowly, thinking there was at least a chance that my conscience would be able to rest at night. *If...if...if.* How many *if*'s do we get in life before we can't sleep at all anymore?

By the time Stan arrived, Peggy had calmed down enough for him to put her through some gentle questioning for ten minutes or so, squatting on his haunches at eye level so as not to distress her even more. What did she hear, feel, or smell that night? What was the weather like? Were there lights on in any of the other houses? What time was it? The one subject he didn't touch on was what she was doing on Arboretum grounds after dark. He spared her that embarrassment.

"It was raining," Peggy said. "It started to rain as soon as I left the house. Not a real hard rain, but enough so that we were hurrying." She blushed. "I didn't smell anything except the bog. That always smells, you know? Like rotting stuff. And we heard the owls again. Kevin said it was funny, but it wasn't. It was spooky, you know?"

Stan patted the back of her hand. "Now think real carefully about those lights. We've been door to door around here, but nobody seems to have been awake or heard a thing."

She shook her head. "There weren't any lights. I'm sure of it."

"Now, when you first went into the teahouse, did you feel like there was anyone else there?"

She moved her feet around in the leaves, staring at them, while she tightened her grip on my hand. "Not at first. But Kevin tripped over something and dropped the flashlight... I don't know...in the dark, it felt like boogey men were everywhere. You know? It was like creepy things were crawling all over me."

I thought about the huge spider webs and knew she had been there before that night. Spiders would have been my first thought, with or without two bodies under my feet, but only if I had known about them ahead of time.

"Can I go now? My dad will have a fit if I don't

have my homework done by the time he gets home."

Stan handed Peggy one of his cards. "Do you carry a cell phone, sugar?"

"No, sir," she said. "We don't believe in cell phones."

I unclipped mine from my belt. "Here, take this one. You'll have it if there's an emergency, and you'll be able to talk to me anytime. I've got a second one at home."

Peggy put her hands behind her back like a child. "I can't. My dad will hear it ringing."

"Not if we set it to vibrate." I showed her how to dial and answer, which seemed to satisfy her. She finally put it in her pocket.

"That's enough for now. Officer Hinton will walk you back. You lock your doors until your daddy gets home, you hear? And tell him I'm gonna want to talk to you again when he's present."

She looked at me with hopeless eyes in a white face, then back at Stan. "Can't you...I mean, my dad has been really down since my mother died. Do you really have to bother him?"

"There's no getting around it, I'm afraid," said Stan. "You're underage and he's your legal guardian."

"It will be all right," I said. *Stupid thing to say.*

"It won't. You don't understand."

Stan said, "What is it we don't understand, Peggy?" And got another torrential flood of tears as a reward for his effort.

I know the human body is made up of more than fifty percent water, but I wouldn't have thought one small teenager could generate that much moisture. Stan finally let her go out of frustration.

"There's something she isn't telling us," I said as we watched Officer Hinton walk her back along the path toward the bog, intending, it seemed, to climb over the vine-covered fence into the Hollowell back yard.

"What makes you say that?"

"I don't know. Something about the way she won't look at you when you ask her questions, especially when she talks about her dad. I can't quite figure her out."

On the other side of a strip of lush Zoysia grass, late-blooming swamp sunflowers swayed in a sudden breeze and a lone hummingbird sampled the salvias. The air was crisp, nature's colors vivid without the humidity of Indian summer. I was aware the instant Ben moved and stood behind me.

Stan said, "Maybe you're having pangs of motherly sympathy. She wouldn't be the first kid whose old man came down hard somewhere around that age. You ever meet the dad?"

"No," I said. "Just talked to him on the phone."

"I did, and once was pleasure enough. Some people like a twenty-four/seven dose of hellfire and damnation. Not my cup of tea, and it wouldn't suit most people, but there's no snake handling or speaking in tongues as far as I've heard. Wife died after a fall a year or so ago. He's probably doing the best he can as a single parent with a teenage girl."

"Still…" I said.

Stan lifted his hat and reset it, always a sign he was ready to be off to something more important. "You aren't thinking she had anything to do with the murders, are you? Because I sure don't see it."

"No, of course not. Can you picture her burying Kevin?"

He shook his head. "Although, I've gotta tell you, I've seen young choir girls who'd rip your heart out for staring at them sideways. Nothing surprises me any more."

"I hate to say it, but what I'm wondering is whether the dad abuses her. You know…spare the rod and spoil the child…that sort of thing. She's way too perfect, yet skittish at the same time. She's scared of him, that's for sure."

"Of course, a heavier hand from your dad might have kept you out of a little trouble. That's another way of looking at it," Stan grunted.

"You old fraud. If Jack Davenport had ever taken a belt to me, you'd have broken his arm."

Stan patted my shoulder. "A little healthy fear, and I do mean a little, never hurt a kid, but you keep your eyes open. She likes you enough to talk to you, so we'll cross that bridge if we need to. Now, I've been gone long enough. Why don't you get on home and cook all your menfolk some supper." He glanced pointedly at Ben.

I swear there's a secret code that men use for silent communication. It would be interesting to know how many millions of years were spent perfecting the technique and why. Could be it was the women who originally wielded the clubs instead of the men.

"Right," I said. "Just keep holding your breath."

We stopped at a restaurant on the way back and bought enough gourmet deli items for an army of menfolk, including a huge chocolate cake to calm the savage beast in all of them if they didn't die of sugar shock first. The four of us, including Randolph and Davis, ate on the dock early enough to catch the glow of the sunset, talking until long after dark while the water lapped against the pilings with soothing regularity.

When the *West Wind* sailed by, heading south under an Australian flag, Davis asked Ben what had happened to his boat.

I looked at Ben over my wine glass. "I'd like to hear that one myself, as long as we're telling stories." *The Three Marys III* was new and expensive, as lovely a sailing vessel as ever tied up at my dock. There was a dandy tale there someplace.

"It's a long story," Ben said. "I picked up a crew member in Eleuthra. He was a solid, clean-cut kid, about twenty-five, working his way back home to Norfolk. Said he'd been around boats all his life, and it was no lie. I couldn't fault him on his sailing experience or willingness to work. I asked about drugs, and he gave me permission to search his gear, which I did and found nothing. Even offered to cook dinner and went back ashore to get groceries. I figure anything he brought on board came in at the bottom of a grocery sack, unless it got tossed to him from another boat."

I sat and listened with my feet on the rail, suspecting where the story was going, surprised he had been careless enough to let drugs slip past him. He must have been desperate for a cooked meal by then. But I was enjoying the sound of his voice and said nothing.

"We sailed generally northeast for another day before we were boarded coming in to Harbor Island by both Customs and the Royal Bahamas Defence Force. Sure enough, when they searched his cabin they brought a kilo of cocaine up on deck. I was floored, but it was there, and it was my boat."

"No," I said. "They didn't?"

"What?" Davis said.

"I'm guessing they confiscated his boat and threw Ben in jail."

"Who's telling this story?" Ben asked. "Anyway the kid's looking at some serious jail time in a part of the world where you don't want to be in jail, so he's doing his best to claim the cocaine belongs to me. I'm there with an expensive new boat—what's not to suspect? In the resulting confusion, we both get the bars slammed in our faces."

"I'd pay good money for a picture of you in jail," I laughed.

He shook his head as if the bemusement were still fresh. "Not even you would laugh about this jail. I didn't see rats, but the cockroaches were probably big enough to scare them away, and the food not fit for either species. I wasn't allowed to make phone calls, but I could write letters—for all the good it did me."

"Couldn't you let the Bureau sort it out?"

"I wasn't part of the Bureau anymore, remember? Not since August."

"Surely someone would have vouched for you."

"There was an old Bureau ID in my wallet, which made the authorities suspicious, even though my other papers were in order. Of course, it didn't help at all that the kid's passport was forged. By then, I was getting more than a little worried. As a last resort, I even had them call my former boss. You remember Lorna?"

I chuckled. "Oh, yes, I've had the privilege. And what happened next?"

"I think you can guess."

"She said she'd never heard of you. That isn't hard to figure."

"I never expected it, and still can't figure out what kind of mix-up occurred."

"She was in love with you. Hell hath no fury and all that."

"No," he said. "You said that in the spring. I still don't believe it."

"Trust me, I know about these things. Get back to the boat. What happened to it?"

His expression was wry. "As far as I know, it's still sitting in the marina under official lock and key. I hustled on home intending to surprise you."

"You left your boat for me?"

I saw Randolph smile in the faded light. I'd thought he was half asleep, but the possibility that another male might be responsible for me made his ears perk up.

Ben said, "Yeah, but lately I've been having second thoughts. A certain someone doesn't seem very appreciative that I thought enough of her to abandon the boat and even get blisters on her behalf. I had to pull strings right and left to get myself on Vitelli property."

It was my turn to smile. "Yes, she is. Now go on. We want to hear the rest."

"As a last resort, I had the authorities get in touch with Stan Council. It wasn't until he got involved that things began to move. I understand he had a few choice words for the director.

"I flew into Raleigh-Durham on Wednesday

morning, intending to drive on down to Wilmington, but Stan called me in the airport right after he heard you were leaving for Hillsborough and why. I rented a car and hightailed it over, calling in favors with contacts at the Bureau while I drove. As it turned out, they were already keeping an eye on Arthur and his new friends, and were only too happy to know what was going on. It was the Bureau connection that convinced Parker Funeral the grave needed a little fine-tuning. It was as close as I could get."

And Stan didn't know I hadn't received Ben's letter, or even that I thought he was missing.

"Why didn't you just call and say, *Pick me up in Raleigh on your way?*"

"What would you have said? I'm guessing you would have told me to butt out."

I started to object, and then reconsidered. Maybe those would have been my very words, knowing how he felt about my association with Sam.

"Besides, you weren't answering your cell phone."

Davis said, "When do you think you'll go get *The Three Marys?*"

"You have any free time coming up?"

"No, sir. Not until Thanksgiving, and I don't know much about sailboats."

"I need to go sooner than that. We'll see what we can do. Maybe you can fly down and sail partway back."

"Your grades are good," said Randolph. "I don't

see why you can't take two or three days off school. We'll call it an educational trip."

Davis was jubilant. "That'd be cool. Wait until I tell the guys."

"All's well that ends well." Randolph rose to his feet and stretched. "Glad to see you aren't rotting in jail somewhere, son."

Ever so casually, Ben said, "Thanks. What about you, Carroll? Want to come along?"

Sometimes you know instantly when an answer is important. I could tell by his hooded gaze and the stillness of his body.

"The whole way?"

"As much as you like."

"Yes," I said. "I think I can manage that."

We sat on for a while longer, listening to the ocean roar in the distance and the tide talk in soft ripples. It was a peaceful, coastal rhythm that can steal over strangers and bind them forever. I wondered if Ben could feel it.

Chapter Twenty-one

I went to bed early in a long flannel knit gown with every intention of going right to sleep. Ben was safely at the end of the hall, by my own choice, and since I was falling asleep on my feet, I didn't think about it much one way or another.

But sleep was hard to come by. The temperature in my room alternated between being too warm and too cool, and every time my eyelids grew heavy, the feeling that I'd overlooked something important came rushing back. It could have been anxiety or the caffeine in the chocolate cake. It could also have been *because* Ben was sleeping down the hall.

Earlier in the evening, I phoned Johnny again and vibrated him awake. He was irritable, and told me everything was peaceful, or would be, if I would stop calling. Lucille and my grandmother had the same answer when I checked in with them. Finally, a little after midnight, I decided the vague anxiety might be about Peggy, but there was little I could do at this time of night without making things harder for her.

Without turning on lights, I let myself out of the house and walked barefoot down the hill to the dock. There are no streetlights on Bald Eagle Lane. It's a neighborhood where good manners have always dictated that dock lights are turned off early. Electricity spoils the view of a night sky, not to mention the reflection of a full moon rising over Rich Inlet.

I cocooned myself with a warm blanket in a corner of the built-in bench, breathing in the heavy smell of salt marsh and ocean breeze. A short distance up the Intracoastal Waterway, a milepost marker winked its red light. I closed my eyes, feeling the primitive, tranquilizing pull of my surroundings, knowing full well that if I fell asleep and the breeze died, mosquitoes and noseeums would eat me for a midnight snack. Despite the risk, I sat on. The moonless night was too beautiful to do otherwise. With winter fast approaching, there might not be another chance to enjoy the stars until springtime.

Footsteps vibrated on the wooden pier. An indistinct shape, just discernable in the starlight, moved like a faint apparition in my direction. Thoughts of Arthur and the Hillsborough attacker flickered at the back of my mind. Unless I went over the side of the railing, there was nowhere to go except into the boat, and I had no key with me. The water was still pushing eighty degrees, but if the tide was out, going over the rail might mean a broken leg or neck.

Before my head stopped processing alternatives, I recognized the gait, even the cadence of the footfalls.

Ben Satterwhite sat down inches away. "What are you doing out here?"

In the dark, I thought he wore jeans and a black sweatshirt, which gave his hands, face, and bare feet the slightest phosphorescent glow.

"I couldn't sleep," I said.

He laughed softly in the dark. "Serves you right."

I said nothing, and after a silence, he tried again. "Did you imagine you couldn't be heard creeping through the house, opening and closing doors?"

"I did, actually."

"Not a chance," he said. "Not when I was aware of every move you made, every time you wiggled in your bed."

I smiled and nudged him with my cold toes. "You're lying. From three doors away? Not even *your* ears are that sharp."

"I must have dreamed it, then, along with all the other things."

The splash of fish sounded nearby, a bluefish maybe, and a sudden scurry of silver minnow tails fled across the water.

"You didn't come down here to seduce me, did you, Ben?"

"I came to make sure you were safe." He let the words hang for a moment. "But if you insist, I could be persuaded without much effort."

I ignored the bait. Instead, I got up and moved to the railing where I leaned my arms on the rough wood, staring east at the black outline of Figure Eight Island. The hem of my long gown flapped against my ankles, wet and cold from the dew-laden grass.

His breath stirred against my ear before I realized he was behind me. In a voice so low I almost missed it, he said, "You're going to be the death of me yet."

He moved the blanket from my shoulders without hurry, giving me, I thought, plenty of time to dissent.

I shivered.

He lifted my hair and put his lips on the back of my neck. Arms encircling my waist from behind felt like summer sand, languorous and irresistible.

I remembered this—remembered everything about him. The way he smelled, the way he moved his lips, his hands, his body. I had even recognized his footsteps in the dark. Smiling, I closed my eyes, and felt his breathing increase.

His hands were in my hair again, lifting, fanning it out with slow fingers so the wind caught it, wafting it around my face. It was the most indescribable sensation, an erotic burst of voltage that I felt all the way to my toes and everywhere in between.

He still hadn't kissed me, and I remember thinking that when he did, it might be necessary to drag us both overboard to get him to stop.

Those hands were still rough from the digging in Hillsborough, yet they knew when to slow and when to speed, causing goose bumps to rise on my upper arms. I was susceptible to every stroke, every whisper, every touch.

He covered my ears with his palms, the false roar

of the ocean in his hands, and turned me slowly. I could feel the chill of the boards beneath my bare feet, the warmth of his mouth wandering, on and on until I was mindless, until I thought I might float with the tide and not return.

But he was moving away, kissing me hard on the lips.

"Stay here," he cautioned in a whisper, and left running toward the house.

Only then did I see the lights at the top of the hill—headlights somewhere in the driveway.

Chapter Twenty-two

I'd reached the crest of the hill when I heard a heavy whumping explosion coming from the front of the house. Flames shot up higher than the roofline. I was certain the garage was on fire.

Male voices suddenly began shouting. I heard an engine roar to life and tires squeal on the driveway as Max started barking like a trained attack dog. Into this pandemonium, a shotgun blast reverberated in the night air.

I don't like shotguns or anything about them. My father was killed by one, and I get nauseous just thinking about them. They are capable of causing the most terrible violence up close and a great deal of damage at medium range. I rushed around to the front of the house—not a very smart thing to do with a shotgun going off. Randolph kept one loaded and propped in the corner of his bedroom. I was praying it was his.

A roaring fire and a heavy smell of gasoline brought me to a halt. The Jeep was engulfed in flames, a raging, wild thing, eating at the garage doors and reaching as high as the lower limbs of the live oak. I gaped at the whole scene, lit up like a movie set, including Randolph and Davis running toward the garage where Ben was silhouetted against the fierce light.

There was only one unlocked door, the slider I'd exited earlier. I ran back, grabbed the kitchen fire extinguisher, and came out the front door, thrusting it at Ben, shouting over the roar for Davis to get the one from the boat.

I went in again for the heavy garage extinguisher, where the fire's heat was already penetrating, the flames casting a frightening pattern of live, dancing fingers on the four-year-old Jaguar. It made me realize I might not only lose the Jeep, but also the garage and much of the house if either vehicle exploded.

Damn it, I thought. If Arthur were responsible, I would strangle him with my own two hands.

In a crisis, the brain often behaves like a jumping bean until it begins to settle down. Then and only then did it occur to me that a fire truck with real, honest-to-God firemen would be an expedient thing to have on hand.

It was a hectic five minutes before the Porters Neck fire trucks arrived. Before then, we emptied three extinguishers and used the garden hoses, but achieved little in the way of flame reduction, although the effort probably saved the garage and kept the fire from spreading. When professionals showed up with chemical sprays, it was all over in minutes.

Sometime during the hullabaloo, a sheriff's deputy appeared. He talked to Ben, Davis, and

Randolph, but not to me. No doubt he thought I was an eccentric neighbor in nightclothes rather than the property owner, but I was too tired to care.

We'd been lucky the breeze was off the ocean and not out of the west, although luck is a relative term when your garage front is charred and your Jeep resembles a burned-out convoy in some third world country. On the other hand, I had to consider what might have happened if I'd parked the Jeep inside the garage as I usually did. I didn't even want to think about it. Everything could be repaired or replaced except the limb of the aging live oak that had already been damaged by Hurricane Elizabeth in July. I was maddest, I think, about that.

By the time the fire was out, and the trucks and deputy off to other emergencies, it was one-thirty in the morning. I herded the men into the kitchen and gave them a choice of hot cocoa or something stronger. Ben and Randolph voted for both.

Somehow Davis had singed his eyebrows, giving him an off-kilter look. Judging by the way he couldn't seem to sit still, the whole affair had been the most exciting thing he'd encountered for a while. A firebomb, I was made to understand, could add significantly to your popularity in high school.

The deputy had called Stan, who in turn phoned to let us know a patrol car would be in the neighborhood until daylight. He also said to tell Ben the buzzard had made its flight, which I took to mean Arthur had gotten on the plane in Raleigh. I remember little else from the short conversation except something at the very end, which sounded a lot like, "Can't you people stay out of trouble?"

The men thought the comment was funny. I didn't, considering that I would be the one dealing with the whole mess, the one whose only other vehicle was trapped in the garage, and the one, God help me, who would have to report it all to Payton Gray.

Randolph had a handle on the situation from the very beginning. "I had one ear out for Arthur, you know, and heard this car come in the driveway going real slow. I'm surprised you didn't hear it."

"I couldn't sleep," I said. "I was on the dock."

"Ah," he said, looking from me to Ben, "that explains it."

Ben's face was expressionless, except perhaps for a tug at the corner of his mouth. Not quite like the cat that got the cream, but close enough. Even though I knew a few more minutes of passion wouldn't have been worth the loss of all my possessions, sexual frustration may have had some influence on my disposition. I kicked him under the table.

"Go on," I said to Randolph.

"By the time I got my pants on and the shotgun in my hand, he had the Jeep's hood up. Just when I got halfway across the yard, I heard this whap like he'd thrown something, followed by a big thumping noise. The whole thing just exploded."

"Molotov cocktail," Ben said. "Simplest arson tool in the business. While he was under the hood, he may have been pulling the gas line loose."

Randolph said, "I tell you, he didn't hang around either. He was back in his car and leaving fast. I shined that big old flashlight right in the car window, and damned if he didn't point a gun at me."

"What kind of car?" There was no point now in reminding him he was lucky to be alive.

"Hell," he said. "Just a car. Not big, not little. I guess that makes it mid-sized. And don't ask me the color. Like I told the deputy, all I know is that it was something dark—any color between red and black— because I damned well wasn't checking close. All I saw was the flames and the gun, but I'll tell you one thing for sure, whatever kind of color we're talking about is gonna be full of buckshot—tag and all."

Ben said, "Wonder why he didn't shoot?"

Randolph lifted his shoulders and chugged the rest of his brandy in one swallow. He avoided my eyes. Davis saw it, too. I could tell by the amazement on his face.

"Dear God," I said. "Lucille is going to kill me." *Not to mention my grandmother.*

"What am I missing here?" Ben looked around the table.

I could feel the goose bumps rising on my arms. "Tell him, Randolph."

He took a deep breath and looked across the table at Ben. "He did shoot. I saw the flash from the gun.

Must have been about the exact same time the shotgun went off. That's why you didn't hear it."

Ben made a whistling sound through his teeth.

"Wow," Davis said, the look on his face showing new respect.

I leaned over and kissed Randolph on his stubbly cheek. "Don't ever take a chance like that again, not for the house, the Jeep, or me. Not for anything."

"I'll try," he said in a voice that carried more than a little pride and not a whit of repentance.

Ben said, "But it wasn't Arthur driving the car?"

"No, it wasn't. He looked damned familiar, but it sure wasn't Arthur."

"He could still have been somebody Arthur hired," Davis said.

I turned over a sheet of dirty, water-stained notebook paper lying in the center of the kitchen table. "I'm not so sure. Take a look at this. If Arthur is responsible, he's a hell of a fast worker. It looks like the same message spray-painted on the walls of the Harbor Island job around ten or eleven Thursday night. And charming Arthur had no idea in advance that Sam was going to show up at my door."

"What have you got there?" Ben said.

Neatly printed with a felt-tip marker, in black caps, were the words: *BITCH – MIND YOUR OWN BUSINESS.* Pretty self-explanatory, if I had only known what business we were talking about.

"Don't touch it," Ben said. "Where did you get this?"

"Tucked under the front doormat. I saw it early on, but thought it was one of those neighborhood flyers for a lost cat, or a kid wanting lawn work. By the time I picked it up thinking it was trash, it had been stepped on a dozen times."

"I'll take it," Ben said, and found a large brown envelope in a cubbyhole of the kitchen desk.

There was nothing else we could do until morning, so I sent Randolph and Davis home, shotgun and all, too tired to get up and see them out. Ben sat on across the table from me with red-rimmed eyes and a nasty burn on the back of his right hand. He looked as exhausted as I was.

I said, "This tops my all-time record for a hot Friday night date. How about yours?"

He laughed. "It started out pretty well."

"It did, indeed."

"I trust you won't go wandering around outside on your own again tonight?"

"Not tonight, no. I've learned my lesson."

"We'll see about that," he said.

I neatened the kitchen and locked up, taking my time, knowing I wouldn't fall asleep soon. I even took the coward's way out and left a message on Payton Gray's answering machine. He wouldn't have believed me anyway. It was another thirty minutes before I'd showered and washed the stench of gasoline smoke from my hair.

He was waiting outside the bathroom when I

finished—bandaged, clean, smelling of soap and virility. Initially, I thought the sight of his bare chest was about as much stimulation as I could handle in my exhausted state.

But then, you'd also have thought I would have had enough of flames for one night.

Chapter Twenty-three

Saturday started out the same as all the other days that week—going from bad to worse. Well, perhaps not exactly like the others. I slept until eight o'clock after waking the first time around six, my usual rising time. Habits are hard to break, even on Saturday. Ben catnapped with one ear on the alert for any movement, which was nice in a naughty kind of way, and the only genuinely good thing to happen all day.

When I woke the second time, there were noises coming from the direction of the kitchen. I padded out in a short robe and found Ben flipping pancakes on the griddle.

He was concentrating so hard that he flipped one on the floor when I stopped behind him. He turned, put both arms around me, and murmured good morning into the neckline of my robe.

I raised his head and kissed him with feeling. "Your pancakes are burning."

"You look deliciously tousled." He was shirtless and barefoot, wearing the same tan Dockers as the day before.

"And *you* just look delicious, but I'm…"

His arms tightened. "You're what?"

"I'm starving."

"We can fix that," he said, and scooped me up with the spatula still in his hand.

"Put me down, you fool," I laughed. "I meant I'm starving for pancakes."

We got as far as the middle of the kitchen, him nibbling on my neck, when his face froze.

My grandmother stood in the doorway.

I don't know which of us was the most surprised, but I'm guessing it was Eleanor Monroe, since she wasn't in the habit of running into men at my house.

"Gran," I said. "We didn't hear you come in."

"I should have knocked."

"No, of course not. Come in. We were just cooking pancakes."

Her lips twitched. "Yes, I can see that." The smell of scorched flour, eggs, and milk permeated the air.

My cheeks burned thinking about what she might have found if she'd arrived two minutes later.

I cleared my throat. "You remember Ben."

He set me hastily on my feet.

"Ah, the missing Mr. Satterwhite. How good to know you're back in town."

"Mrs. Monroe. It's a pleasure to see you again."

"Really?" she said and laughed out loud. "Young man, go put a shirt on before I have a heart attack. By the time you get back, we'll all have composed ourselves."

"Yes, ma'am," he said grinning, and left the room so fast it was almost comical.

"What are you doing here this early?" I asked, straightening my robe.

"Lucille and I heard you had some trouble last night. We came to see for ourselves if you were all OK, and I'm happy to say that you seem to be recovering well. And, please, this is your home, so wipe that guilty look off your face. Do you think your grandfather and I never canoodled in the kitchen?"

Canoodled? "He isn't exactly Grandfather."

She fanned herself. "No, my dear girl, he most *definitely* is not."

I may not have known who was the most surprised, but I could spot who was having the most fun, and it wasn't me. This would be a prize-winning, salacious tidbit at her card games. By the time she and Lucille finished embellishing the story, it would be a favorite tale among a hundred eighty-somethings in town. Before it was over, busy tongues would have us rolling naked on the kitchen floor.

"Carroll, you should see the look on your face. Get some clothes on and you'll feel better. Really. And don't forget how old I am. In fifteen minutes, I may have forgotten everything." One of the most refined women in Wilmington began to chuckle and then to laugh, which started Charlie cackling, so that by the time I closed the door to my room, it sounded as if a flock of partying magpies had invaded the kitchen.

I pressed both palms to my forehead and took a deep breath.

When the door opened, Ben entered, already dressed and knotting a blue tie on a starched white shirt. He was laughing, too.

"Stop that," I said crossly. "Haven't you caused enough trouble?"

What I got for my effort was a noteworthy, lingering kiss that backed me against the wall and jellified my knees. He finished with a last kiss on my nose and disappeared before I regained my wits.

Truly, the man had no shame. But he had put on a shirt and tie for my grandmother. We would see, I thought, just how far he got matching wits with her.

I dressed in a hurry, pulling on jeans and a high-necked sweater set, although Gran had likely gotten a good look at the bruises earlier. Sooner or later she would want to know how they got there, and I'd better have a decent story ready.

In the hallway I gave myself a lecture about being thirty years old and able to handle one tiny, elderly woman. The man was a whole different problem. Him I wasn't so sure about.

She was sitting at the table with Ben when I made my reappearance, debating the merits of flavoring maple syrup with rum or bourbon. It sounded like a North-South thing to me, but they settled on rum in an amicable manner. Brownie points were being scored right and left, none of which were being awarded to me.

Ben was Emeril in a white shirt, making fresh coffee and perfect pancakes. I didn't know about my grandmother, who left the cooking to Lucille, but *I* was impressed.

We were almost finished eating when I said, "What else did Randolph tell you at the crack of dawn?"

She stopped with her fork raised. "Only that you had another friend visiting in town. I thought you might take me with you when you go over this morning."

I tried for an innocent expression. "You mean visit Jinks Farmer?"

"Lucille and I can manage Jinks on our own, thank you. I'll pick her up at Randolph's after we finish. You know who I mean."

That explained the garden club dress early on a Saturday morning.

"Let me make sure I do. You want to visit with Sam Vitelli? Did you hear that, Ben?"

"No." He grinned. "I'm not listening."

She beamed at him and offered more syrup. "We've talked on a number of occasions. I want to meet the man, that's all."

"A number of occasions? Define the number."

"Carroll, don't be naïve. You know I talked to him before you married Daniel, and afterward, we just continued to chat from time to time. Don't look so astonished. I'm sure there are other things you don't know about me."

I was beginning to wonder. "Really? Like what?"

She waved a dismissive hand. "I just think it's time I saw for myself what kind of man he is."

It was too early for my brain to come up with a good reason to keep her away from Sam without letting her know about Arthur and his threats. If we used her car and went the back way along Futch Creek Road…

"All right, you're on," I said, and watched Ben's eyebrows go up. "Let me call Johnny first and see how Sam is doing."

Johnny said Sam was doing better after a ton of sleep. They were waiting for Jackie to get the results of a few remaining blood tests. Sam was even talking about leaving Nixon Davis.

"Don't let him," I said.

"Not to worry," Johnny said. "He isn't going anywhere if I can help it. If necessary, I'll have Jackie run some complicated tests to stall him, but we'll manage it."

"Ask him if he's feeling up to a couple of female visitors." So he was already in collusion with Jackie, was he? That was good.

"Hold on a minute," he said, and mumbled a few words with his hand over the mouthpiece before coming back. "We'll be ready. Give him half an hour or so to finish dressing."

"We won't stay long. Tell him my grandmother wants to finally meet him."

At the nursing home, we found Sam had been whisked away to repeat one of the tests. We waited in the lobby where Gran would be comfortable and able to chat with friends. One extended conversation seemed set to last for an hour, and when I spotted Jackie rounding a corner, I made my escape. Over my shoulder, I saw Ben settle into the next chair with the *New York Times*.

I caught up with Jackie outside a patient's door.

She said, "He looks better this morning. I hear he slept through the night. That's a good sign."

"He's a clever old dog, so don't necessarily believe him. Johnny says he's talking about leaving."

"Mr. Rinaldi and I have an understanding, so rest your mind on that one."

I smiled at her. "Good. Did you find anything else?"

"There is one possibility. We're repeating a blood test this morning to be sure. And no, we found nothing to indicate a heart problem. On the contrary, he seems to be remarkably fit for a man in a state of collapse. I can't give you the details, but I'm sure Mr. Rinaldi will fill you in. He sits in on all our discussions."

"Then I'll go find Johnny, instead of keeping you from your patients. Thank you for everything you're doing."

As she slid through the doorway, she put her head around the corner. "I saw you come in with your grandmother and that handsome hunk. You don't look like you got much sleep yourself, so I know you have better things to do. Go home, why don't you, and leave all the worrying to the experts. It's what we're paid for."

The door closed softly, leaving me standing in the bright hallway wondering if I had a big S for *sex* branded on my forehead.

I had to look down three more halls before I found Johnny. If Sam had slept well, he must have made a lot of noise, because Johnny had dark circles under his eyes.

I said, "Jackie says she may have found something you might share with me. Would Sam mind, do you think?"

"She thinks he may be overdosing on Hytrin, causing dizziness, a racing heart, and low blood pressure. I think I got that right."

"Is he?"

He shook his head. "Not unless he's hiding prescription bottles around the house. I've handled the medications for years. When I don't nag, he forgets to take anything, so I'm not buying the overdose theory. If he was getting too much, Arthur was behind it. You can bet your last dollar."

"How dangerous is it?"

"Depends on the dose. Enough and it could cause

him to go into shock or his blood pressure to drop too low."

"Nice fellow, our Arthur. What are we going to do?"

"You aren't going to do anything."

"Does Sam know?"

"Oh, yes. And we'll take care of it."

"Johnny…"

"Sam knows how to handle it. You don't have to worry."

"I will, though," I said. "We'll be in the lobby when he's ready."

Ben was still engrossed in the paper, and Maude Akers was winding down. Gran seemed relieved to see me.

"It won't be long," I said when Maude left.

"For a woman on oxygen, she can get a lot of words out between breaths."

I laughed. "Why do you think I abandoned you?"

"Before I forget, I have a message from Lucille. She said to tell you her sources have nothing interesting to report about your Reverend Hollowell. His Church of the Faithful seems to be strict, but that isn't so unusual in the Bible belt."

"It probably isn't important. No doubt, every teen thinks at least one parent is mean. I thought the same thing myself."

"If she's as bad as you were, I feel sorry for the

Reverend. The best thing to be said for the teen years is that you only have to survive them once."

"True, but I wasn't that bad. Was I?"

"You could have been worse, I suppose, but I couldn't see how at the time. I might still have red hair if it hadn't been for you."

I laughed. Lucille usually had more to say—that I'd been the original model who gave the whole age group a bad name.

"I remember her mother," Gran said, "although how she could work for a man with such a terrible comb-over, I don't know."

It was sometimes hard to follow Gran's conversation patterns. She could be talking about Maude Akers or picking up on a discussion we'd had two days before. I took a stab. "Peggy's mother?"

"Isn't that who we're talking about?"

"It doesn't matter now."

"Bill," she said. "Bill Burris."

"What did you say?"

"I said it was Bill Burris."

"What about him? Don't you remember he was the murdered man in the teahouse Tuesday morning?"

"Of course. Why on earth would I forget? I'm simply trying to tell you that's who Peggy Hollowell's mother used to work for."

"There are a hundred and sixty-five thousand people in this county," I said. "How could you know that?"

Her mouth formed a mysterious smile. "I have an army of secret sources, every single one of them with sharp eyes and excellent hearing."

I looked at Ben and back at an eighty-six-year-old woman that no one would have ever thought to question. "Gran, this could be important. Are you sure Lynn Hollowell worked for Bill Burris?"

"When you asked the other day, I forgot I met her once at a candidate's rally. And Lucille's first cousin, Alma, is friends with Mary Whittaker, whose company cleaned the Burris offices. I think they had a thing going for a while, not that I want to gossip about a dead woman, but otherwise, why would Mary and Alma have told Lucille about it in the first place?"

Why, indeed? I was still trying to take it all in. "Lynn Hollowell and Bill Burris?"

"You know Lucille is never wrong."

Another time I might have laughed, because it was truer than I liked to think. "Excuse me for one minute. I'll be right back."

Ben took one look at my face and put the *New York Times* aside. He caught up with me in the corridor. "What's wrong?"

"Everything…or maybe nothing. I'm not sure. Come down to the end of the hall with me. I have to call Stan and I don't want Gran to hear."

I punched his home number in with shaky fingers. "Please," I said out loud. "Don't let the machine pick up."

Stan's wife, Opal, answered on the sixth ring and, recognizing my voice, said, "Well, hello, stranger girl. Where on earth have you been hiding yourself?"

"Just busy," I said. "I've missed you, too. Listen, I don't mean to be rude, but I need to talk to Stan right away. I think he said he was off this weekend. Do you know where I can find him?"

"It's a miracle. For once I do know. He's raking leaves in the back yard. Hold on a minute."

Ben said, "What's going on?"

"Don't go away. I'll fill you in as soon as…"

Stan said in my ear, "I hate leaf raking. This better be damned important enough to get me out of it."

"Give me two minutes. Remember Peggy Hollowell's mother died about a year ago?"

He grunted something unintelligible.

"Did you know she worked for Bill Burris and may even have had an affair with him?"

"Gossip?"

"Lucille's cousin is a friend of the woman who cleaned Bill's office."

"It's gossip."

"Maybe, maybe not. Peggy keeps saying that we don't understand but won't tell us why, and it just occurred to me that when she says her father has been sick, she might be talking about mental illness. I'm getting the creepy feeling there may have been something not quite right about the mother falling down the stairs."

There was a long silence on the other end. A cell phone rang and out of the corner of my eye, I watched Ben turn his back and put it to his ear.

Stan said, "It's a hell of a jump from accidental death to a man of the cloth murdering three people."

I thought I had his attention and tried to lob a clincher. "I think Peggy could be in danger. What if Hollowell killed his wife and Burris, Liz Hunter because she was with him that night, and Kevin in case he recognized him? Peggy knows, or at least suspects him. I'm sure of it."

He laughed. I hate it when he laughs at me.

"You're reaching, girl. Way, way out. You know that. There was nothing to indicate violence that I remember. I have a vague recollection that one of the paramedics told me he smelled bourbon on Lynn Hollowell. Seems like the wife was in the hospital a while before she died of a blood clot on the brain or something. There was no reason to bring in law enforcement—nothing whatsoever to indicate foul play."

"Stan, what if…"

"Before you get so far into this that you embarrass yourself, I want you to back your boat up a minute and listen. We tracked down the homeless fellow who's been sleeping in the Arboretum, one Rusty Waltmoor. Seems he's wanted in Orlando for assault. When we picked him up this morning, he had a loaded gun in his pack, which he says he *found* on Monday night. You want to take a wild stab at whether there's gonna be a bullet match and whose prints are on the gun?"

"Whose?"

"Only Rusty's. Now, you see how easy it is to careen down the wrong trail?"

If I wanted to frame a homeless man, or anyone else for that matter, leaving him the murder weapon would be a good way to do it. I sighed. So much for theories. Even I knew it was far more likely that Stan had arrested the right man.

"On another matter, the Ruggiero brothers claim they were all in Jacksonville at a bar Saturday night. Nobody remembers them, and they don't know what time they got home. We're still checking with the Jacksonville police, but I don't have enough yet to search the Ruggiero property. In my book, we're looking at the three of them for Jinks, the vandalism, and the firebombing."

"I had a run-in with Danny Ruggiero yesterday."

"What happened?"

"He threatened me. Fortunately, Randolph and Ben were there."

"You be careful, you hear. You saw what kind of damage a two-by-four could do. You want to be in the same situation Jinks was in? I can always pick him up if the threat was specific enough."

"No. Unfortunately, I don't think it was."

"Then watch yourself. I'll see if a background check turns up anything on the three brothers."

"Stan, even if it's only abuse…"

"Hush now about Peggy. I can't do my job based on supposition. You know I can't. I'll make a couple of calls to social services and get back to you. How's that?" His patience was ebbing.

"I apologize for disturbing your Saturday."

"You can disturb all you want, girl, but it isn't going to change the facts, now is it?"

Three feet away, Satterwhite was scribbling something on a piece of paper.

Ben handed me the note as I made one last attempt to convince Stan. "You're the one who taught me to be suspicious of coincidences. Look at it from that end. The wife is dead, the lover is dead, and three bodies are found almost in his back yard, leaving only his daughter as a possible witness."

I waited while he thought about it. Ben made a pointing motion at the note.

"Coincidences are funny things," Stan said. "Sometimes they really are just random unrelated events that look coincidental only because you've linked them together into flawed categories. I'm not saying you aren't on to something about abuse, but you've left out one other noteworthy person who might account for both the firebombing and the attack on you in Hillsborough. He might even be responsible for Jinks."

"You're talking about Arthur. It couldn't have been him last night, unless he hired someone to do it."

"Well, that's my whole point, honey. You don't have any way of knowing that."

"You're wrong. Ben just got a phone call. Arthur has been missing since nine o'clock last night. Somebody used a truck to try to ram his car into the Hudson River."

Chapter Twenty-four

Stan said. "Talk about narrowing your feasibility list. Does Vitelli know about this?"

"Not yet. He's off having blood redrawn or something."

"Now, don't get all huffy with me, but do you think he had a hand in Arthur's disappearance?"

"No," I said. "Johnny maybe, but the list of possible suspects may have gotten bigger lately. Sam said he was making deals with sharks."

"What happened?" he asked.

"Ben knows. Hold on." I handed the phone over to him.

He listened while Stan talked, with an occasional "yes, uh huh," and then, "Not so good. It was a bad wreck, less than an hour after his plane landed." Ben made additional grunts, gave a shrug and a final, "No problem." He handed the phone back to me with an amused look on his face that meant they had talked about me.

"Carroll?" Stan said.

"I'm back." I was still eyeing Ben.

"All right. I'm gonna verify some things. You sit tight until I get back to you. I don't want you running off like a guinea hen looking for trouble. Pay attention to Ben. He knows what to do."

"What did you say to him? He looks like a stand-up comic with new material."

"Ask him. But be nice."

"Don't count on it," I said into a dead phone and raised my eyebrows at Ben. "Well? Are you going to tell me?"

He loosened the blue tie. "Paraphrased, I'm to keep you out of trouble if I have to tie you to the bed and see if I can come up with some way to keep your…mind occupied."

"He said that, did he? My mind? So now you're making not-so-veiled references to my pathetically limited love life over cell phones?"

Ben winced, but his merriment was plain. "From the look on your face, I don't think his suggestion will be an option."

I was glad someone found it funny.

"No. It will not." My voice was cool. I had a number of choice words ready to roll off the tip of my tongue, all of which were better left unsaid. He was saved by the appearance of Johnny pushing Sam's chair.

Ben nodded politely, but remained in the hallway as if being in the same room with the two of them would be contaminating.

Sam said, "We met your remarkable grandmother in the lobby. I see now where your charm and beauty originated. She seemed surprised to see I did not have two heads and that I was temporarily a Monroe, but she managed to be gracious nonetheless. What a pity Isabella never had the pleasure."

"I'm amazed my ears weren't burning."

He laughed as I held the door open for the chair.

As it closed behind us I said, "Sam, I'm afraid we have some bad news about Arthur. There was an accident after he left Newark Airport last night. A truck rammed his car somewhere near the Hudson River."

They turned their eyes toward me. There was something there I couldn't read—not sorrow, guilt, or even self-reproach. And it wasn't surprise either. The closest I could come was *acknowledgment*—the judgment of the jungle, what goes around comes around. I thought of old Malay proverbs about not giving salt to the rain or flowers to swine, and had the feeling that only Arthur's mother would weep for him.

They didn't ask me how I knew.

Sam said, "How bad is it?"

"I don't know. Serious, I think, and possibly not an accident. There was blood in the vehicle. The keys were in the ignition, but Arthur is missing."

Seconds went by before Sam passed a hand over his face. "I tried on a number of occasions to warn him he was aligning himself with the worst of the worst, making deals with people who have no principles and less integrity than hyenas."

Johnny said nothing.

"I'm sorry," I said, putting a hand on Sam's shoulder. "I never got to know him well, but he's part of your family. Your sister must be devastated at the news."

Johnny's mouth twisted. "She should be, seeing as she encouraged him. If she..."

Sam said sharply, "Johnny!"

"Does this mean you'll be going back soon?" I asked.

"No," they answered in unison, with Sam suddenly looking white and exhausted again.

As soon as good manners permitted, I began to make my exit. At the last minute, Sam caught my hand and held it. There was the barest sheen of moisture in his eyes. "Arthur is not all bad, you know. As a child he was like a young prince with charm, agility, and intellect to spare. We indulged both Daniel and Arthur more than we should have—the way people do with exceptional children. Instead, we should have taught both of them more about how hard it is to maintain integrity. There comes a time, though, when grown men are what they make of themselves."

I kissed him on the temple. "Grown men and women are always responsible."

Wisdom comes mostly from old wounds. It took me a long time to learn that everything happening to me wasn't my responsibility or even something I could always have influence over.

We talked a few minutes longer, but it was obvious he wanted me to go. "Get some more rest," I said. "I'll stop by later in the day."

"Johnny will be here."

I paused at the door. "Will you do me a favor?"

"Of course, if I can."

"Don't think about leaving until Jackie says so."

Down the hall Ben commented, "I never thought I'd be hearing a Vitelli give a lecture on integrity."

"You were listening at the door?"

"Couldn't help it. Voices carry."

I stopped, staring at him, feeling something tight forming in my chest.

"Be quiet," I said, much harsher than I meant it to sound. "I've had enough of your harping about Sam when you don't even know him. You need to get over this, because he's part of my history and my present. It won't be necessary for you to like him, socialize, or even cast eyes on him if it affronts your lily-white Bureau heart. And if you find it offensive to *just do it for me*, we can no doubt come to some kind of future understanding. It will make me miserable, though, and if I'm unhappy, you'll be doubly so, and that's as clear as I think I can make it. So what do you say? Can you work with me on this or shall we shake hands—right here, right now?"

This is where he gives up, I thought. *This is where he walks away.* I felt a sudden sense of loss and panic.

"Are we going to have a future?"

"I don't know, Ben. Are we?"

"If we do, you're going to be inflexible as hell on

some issues, aren't you? And Vitelli is going to be one of them."

"Yes, I am. But I make a good friend, too, and I'm worth the effort involved. What's it to be, Ben?"

It seemed a long time before an answer came.

He reached for my hand as if planning to shake it in a business-like parting. At the last second, he raised it to his mouth instead.

"We'll work something out," he said. "You aren't getting rid of me that easily."

Chapter Twenty-five

Once we reached home, I gave the car back to Gran, who walked down to the dock where Randolph and Lucille were fishing, no doubt to tell them what the infamous Sam Vitelli was really like. Ben and I spent ten minutes with a detective from the sheriff's department.

I also checked my answering machine, which in all the excitement of the morning, I had forgotten to do. There were three messages from as many painters, and one from a man wanting the supervisor's job, whose manner and grammar were so offensive I didn't even bother to write his number down.

Lastly, there was a message from Peggy, which only increased my unease. I listened to it twice, with the disquieting sense that time was slipping away, that I would be too late.

"It's me, Peggy," she said over the machine, as if I wouldn't recognize her voice. "I don't want to call the sheriff in case my dad finds out, so can you tell him I think there was a baby crying that night, a little baby. You know—like a new one. Tell him maybe it was Mrs. Hanford's. I've got to go. Bye." There was a lost quality to her voice, as if she had wanted a connection with another human being that couldn't be established by leaving a message.

I dialed her number and listened to it ring without success. If her father answered, I planned to hang up. I played the message again.

"What are you doing?" Ben asked.

"Listening to my messages. Why?" I turned the volume down.

"You're pacing, the same as outside Vitelli's room when you were on the phone with Stan. I'd say you're at the hand-wringing stage."

"I was pacing?"

"Whatever you want to call it when you're stalking back and forth. If you're wound this tight very often, I need to know it ahead of time."

"I'm worried about Peggy. I get like this when something is about to happen—jumpy, anxious—like I'm tingling out of my skin. Don't you dare laugh."

"A strong tranquilizer might help."

I threw a small pillow at his head. It missed and hit the corner of Charlie's cage, causing a flurry of feathers in the air.

"Now see what you made me do."

"Think about it," he said. "If you don't actually *know* something is going to happen, maybe you're just overly apprehensive that it might. You don't see this stuff, do you? Tell me we aren't talking visions here?"

"Is this Bureau Logic 101? Because if it is, I may have to conjure up a vision you aren't going to like much."

He began making spooky Halloween sounds.

"Please stop making jokes, and don't analyze me. Only on rare occasions do I get even a microscopic blip of an image—never enough to truly see anything. It is, however, enough to scare the hell out of me."

"Sorry. But you should see yourself. You're like a woman possessed."

"Thank you for pointing this out, Dr. Logic. And just so you'll have the complete picture, when I get this way I'm wrong less than half the time. If you're as good at math as you are at analyzing, you'll know that more than half the time something *does* happen— not next month or next year, but soon. And there's one last thing. It isn't funny in the least, and neither are you."

"Your latest theory about Hollowell didn't hold water, though, did it?"

"No, I freely admit it. But there's a killer still out there somewhere, which means Peggy is vulnerable."

Both hands went up, signaling surrender, before he reached out and looped a bit of my hair around his fingers. "Are you going to be one of those women who keep a record of the all the stupid things I say?"

"Not yet," I said. "Do you think it'll be necessary?"

He laughed and ran a thumb across my lower lip. "Not so long as you focus on the essentials."

I narrowed my eyes at him. "I'm not easily distracted. You should know that by now. Go find something else to do with your one-track mind so I can get my work done."

While he read the paper, I dialed my cell phone, now in Peggy's possession, letting it ring a full ten times in case she had trouble figuring out the buttons. There was no answer.

Phoning Jinks didn't help. He either wasn't in his hospital room or couldn't answer the telephone.

I neatened the kitchen, and since it doesn't take much to make him sulk for days, talked nicely to Charlie while feeding him peanuts by hand. I even rechecked the garage to be certain there was no way I could get the car out.

Five whole minutes passed before I tried Peggy again. There was still no answer.

Ben, who had already stared over the top edge of the paper two or three times, made a great production of refolding it. "That's it. Let's go. You won't be able to stand still until you've checked on her, so we might as well get it over with."

"I can't just go barging in. What if Hollowell is there? The last thing I want to do is make things worse."

"Then I'll be taking a door-to-door survey or selling magazines, and when we finish with Peggy, we'll go see Jinks. That should settle all your chicks in the nest so you'll be able to relax the rest of the day—unless there's more trouble that I don't know about."

"No," I said.

"Good. So play your cards right, Davenport, and

I might even take you walking on the beach afterward."

"If Peggy has somehow broken both legs, I'll expect a full apology, beach or no beach."

"Fifty dollars says she's at the mall with every other teenager in America on a Saturday morning."

"You're on. Remember, the odds are in my favor."

There was only one way to find out. Anything was better than standing around biting my nails.

We parked down the block from the Hollowell house, a small white two-story with a detached garage toward the back of the lot. From the road, I caught a glimpse of the Arboretum's color as we drove past.

"Pretend you've lost a dog or something," I said. "I just want you to find out if the dad is home and get a glimpse of Peggy if you can."

"Why me? I thought you said you'd never met the guy."

"I haven't, but we've talked on the phone. He might recognize my voice. If he's abusing her, we don't want to give him any more ammunition. I only want to be sure she's all right."

"You realize, don't you, that she may not be answering because she ran your battery down making overseas calls to a pen pal?"

I winced. "Thanks. Still, it won't break the bank and I'll feel a lot better."

"Then, lost dog it is. You think I can handle that?"

"And more if you hold on a second." I reached over, unknotted the blue tie, and slipped it off. The top button unfastened easily, as did the second one. There was an expression close to hunger in his eyes when I hesitated at the third button. I moved on to the sleeves until they were folded midway up his forearms.

"You heartless little tease. You picked a hell of a place."

"Hush," I said, tousling his hair until he looked like he'd sailed all morning in typhoon winds. "Now, you almost look as if you belong around here."

He went first to the house next to Peggy's—a clever ruse, I thought, in case Hollowell was watching. A woman with a baby in her arms came to the door, and I could tell by the coquettish way she tilted her head that he was the most interesting thing to ring her bell in months. It got me wondering if Stan had remembered to check on the woman with the new baby to find out if she'd seen anything the night of the murders.

I watched in the rearview mirror as he cut across her yard and used the Hollowell buzzer.

The door opened, and I caught a glimpse of a man standing in the entrance—just a glimpse—and not even a very good one at that. He was older than Ben, shorter, heavier. When he moved back, Ben stepped over the threshold.

My arms went icy as a cold well formed in the pit

of my stomach. I had the most awful, irrational feeling that I would never see him again.

I was out of the car and running, unsure of why, but certain there was something… A distance of half a block is like a mile when you're panicky. There are no magic legs, no angel wings. I ran, hoping I was wrong.

The front door stood open a few inches as I paused on the porch. I could hear Ben saying, "Sometimes kids notice stray dogs more than adults, so if you wouldn't mind asking your daughter, I would appreciate it. I moved in recently, and I guess Zack just doesn't know how to find his way back to the new house."

The second voice shouted, "Peggy!" in a strong thespian bass. There was a short pause. "She's working on a school project, but she can spare the time. Left it till the last weekend as usual. You know how kids are these days."

Hollowell bellowed her name a second time. I heard feet moving up the stairs. He shouted once more as the voice faded, traveling farther away toward another part of the house. I only caught snatches of words like "*better not,*" "*radio,*" and "*come out here*" before two sets of footsteps returned to the wooden stairs.

Hollowell said, "This man seems to think you might have seen his dog." From the back of the room, no congregation would have trouble hearing his voice.

Ben was closer to the door. "It's a young yellow

Lab, frisky as all get out and loves little kids...you know the kind. He's been missing two days. I sure would hate to lose him."

"No sir," Peggy said. "I haven't seen any stray dogs, but if I do I'll be sure and hold him for you. Which house is yours?"

"Midway on the right in the second block down. Guess that's it, then. I thank you folks for your time."

It's the little things that trip you up when you lie, but I don't know what else Ben could have said. There was no way he could have known the street curved around and ended in a cul-de-sac about six or seven houses from the one in which he was standing. I waited for Hollowell to ask the street number.

Instead he said, "You never told me your name."

"Satterwhite. Ben Satterwhite."

My heart was thumping. There was a sound like wood scraping, like a drawer opening.

In a high-pitched child's voice, Peggy said, "Daddy, what are you doing?"

Hollowell said, "Go back to your room, Peggy. Now!"

"No, Daddy."

"Mr. Hollowell..." Ben began.

"Reverend Hollowell. Do you think I don't recognize you, whatever your name is, or that I don't know every sinner on my own street and where they live?"

Ben must have made a motion toward the front door.

"No, I wouldn't move if I were you. Just keep both feet right where they are because you aren't going anywhere. I was in Desert Storm, in case you're wondering if I can use this."

Peggy began to whimper. As I came through the entrance, she put both hands over her face and squealed behind them, a muffled, pitiful sound.

Hollowell was standing on the second stair from the top with Peggy just behind him. He was unshaven, his shirt fastened unevenly all the way to the top, and he wore a flat, empty expression, like a shock victim. There were dark circles under eyes that bulged with fatigue, and he had the overall look of a man who had seen the hounds of hell.

Ben was near the foot of the stairs, looking at a black revolver pointing down at him. He was maybe eight feet from the threshold and escape.

I didn't think of the consequences. I thought only of Ben.

"What do *you* want?" Hollowell said, with no more surprise than if I'd come to read the water meter. He knew who I was.

Ben's head jerked in disbelief. "Carroll, get the hell out of here."

I tried not to look at him, afraid of what Hollowell might do. "Are you all right, Peggy?"

"My daughter is none of your business," Hollowell said.

"That's true." I tried to keep my voice even,

wondering if I could pretend there was no gun in his hand. "She's a sweet, lovely girl. You've done a good job with her."

His eyes moved in momentary confusion. "Answer her, Peggy."

She held both hands clasped tight to her midriff, where they made twitching motions against her body. Her voice was little more than a cracked breath filled with tension and fear. "I'm…fine. What are you doing here?"

"Giving you a ride to the library so you can finish the research on your project, remember? Are you ready to go?" Not much of a ruse, but it wasn't like I'd had a lot of experience snatching daughters away from fathers with guns.

She wet her lips, glancing from me to Ben and back to her father again. It seemed a long time before she whispered, "Daddy?"

When he said nothing, she waited a few seconds before sliding past him on tiptoes and moving three steps down the stairs. Her hand gripping the railing was white across the knuckles.

"Peggy?"

She froze. "Yes, sir?"

"You aren't going anywhere."

Her legs collapsed under her, and she sat down abruptly, her chin quivering.

I stretched my hand toward her. "Reverend Hollowell, I'm Carroll Davenport, a good friend of your daughter's. You and Peggy are in no danger, so why not let her come with me? There's no need for the gun."

Without emotion, he said, "Peril comes in many disguises."

"Not from me, and you're a man of the cloth. You don't want to hurt anybody else. Why don't you put the gun away so we can sit down and figure out how to help both of you?"

I didn't have any of the trained skills needed for negotiating, and probably not even the temperament, but I knew that above all else I had to keep him calm and talking.

Hollowell's gun was steady on Ben. "I don't know what you're talking about."

"It was you, wasn't it?" I tried to speak in a normal tone although my pulse was racing with apprehension. I could feel the tremor in my voice.

"You're talking in riddles. I repeat…I have no idea what you're talking about."

"Yes, you do," I said. "I recognized you the minute you opened the front door. You were in my hotel room in Hillsborough, and I have the bruises to show for it." I pulled the sweater neck aside just for a moment. He didn't look at the bruises, and I felt a stirring of greater fear overlaid with anger, which wasn't going to help any of us. "You painted black warnings all over the Harbor Island house and beat Jinks Farmer when he walked in on you—left him to die, choking on his own blood. Last night you almost gunned down an old man, a good man, in my driveway. It wasn't enough for you to firebomb my Jeep and try to burn my house down. You had to shoot at one of the best men ever born.

"And why? Because you thought Peggy told me your secret. What I don't understand, though, is why you didn't kill me in Hillsborough. You'd already murdered three other people and gotten away with it."

"Carroll…" Ben tried again.

Hollowell's eyes jerked left and right, as if expecting more visitors from the adjoining rooms. "I should have killed you, but now will do just as well."

I waited for his wild look to ease before saying, "I think you don't really want to hurt anyone else, otherwise Peggy and I would already be dead."

"You don't…know…anything." He closed his eyes for a brief second, rocking on the balls of his feet as if he were about to lose his balance.

Words were my only weapon. I didn't know what else to do. "The first time I saw you was at Laney High the morning I drove Peggy to school. You stood in front of my Jeep in a three-piece suit and glared at me. I thought you were the principal. You must have followed us because Peggy saw you, too. That's why she panicked and ran."

"Did you think I wouldn't see her get in a car with a black boyfriend, in front of my own house for all the world to see?"

I glanced at Peggy. "A friend. A nice kid. There's a difference, and they weren't even sitting together in the same part of the Jeep."

"It doesn't matter. You're whores—all of you. You'll burn in everlasting hell."

"And the murdering minister who kills his own wife? What do you think, Hollowell? Where will he burn if not in the hottest possible part of hell?"

Peggy's face was slick with tears. "He didn't mean to. You're sick, Daddy. Don't you understand?"

"Shut up," he shouted, his face contorted, but he never turned to look at her or moved the gun away from Ben. "She deserved it, carrying on with Burris behind my back as if I wouldn't know—as if God wouldn't tell me about it and how to punish her. Your mother was the biggest harlot of all, and you're just like her, fornicating behind your father's house like an animal. You think I don't know what you were planning to do?"

"No, Daddy…"

I said, "You killed Kevin, too, a sixteen-year-old boy—buried him in the mud so that his own mother wouldn't recognize him."

Peggy made a choking sound.

"He took my daughter to the house of sin. I did what any good father would have done."

Ben made a half turn in my direction.

"Don't! If you move again, I'll kill you."

"Let the women go," Ben said in a calm voice. "I'll

stay, but let them go. You can take my car if you want. I won't try to stop you. I don't even have a gun."

Hollowell didn't answer.

"At least let Peggy leave," I said. "You've already caused her enough torment to ruin her whole life. Think about it. You held her in your hands when she was a baby. She's your own flesh and blood, a living part of you, and even though you took away her mother, she doesn't hate you. You think she told me about your wife, but I give you my word she didn't. In spite of everything you've done, she still loves you enough to protect you. Please, don't hurt her any more."

I took a series of slow steps forward, bringing me within a few feet of Ben, and watched his back muscles tense. I could almost touch him.

Peggy astonished us all by leaping down the stairs and throwing her arms around my waist, holding tight as if certain he would try to pull her away.

"Get back here, Peggy."

She buried her face in my shoulder, refusing to look at him.

"Now!" he said in the coldest, harshest voice I could remember hearing, one that caused her to tremble against me and loosen her grip. I put my own arms around her and held fast.

Ben said, "Reverend, please put the gun down so Peggy won't get hurt."

"That's enough. The time for talking is done." Hollowell started down the stairs too swiftly and lost his balance, sliding the last few steps on his back, stunned by the impact.

It was the moment Ben had been waiting for, except that it came too fast and without warning, catching us all by surprise. I saw him gather himself, moving with speed toward Hollowell, but the gun was still pointing at his chest from no farther away than the length of his own body.

He stopped in mid-stride.

My breath caught somewhere in my throat, my arms hurting with the need to reach out and pull him out of harm's way.

Hollowell was breathing hard. "Get back or I'll kill you," he said to Ben. "I mean it. Peggy, get away from her."

She struggled in my arms. "Daddy, please…"

I've thought a lot about my next words to Hollowell, words that were equally divided into bluff and entreaty, and want to think there was some small measure of humanity in them. I'll never be sure. I was certain of one thing, though—he wasn't getting Peggy if I could help it. "Reverend Hollowell…"

"Shut up!" he said.

"Listen to me. Please listen. You must know that whatever you do—whether you kill one or all of us— there's no possible way you can hide this crime. Not in broad daylight in your own home with the police on the way. I'm begging you. In the name of heaven, find it in your heart to do one good, final thing."

He was silent so long I thought perhaps he was listening, but then a slow sneer began to form on his face.

Ben saw it, too, and twisted his body toward me in a long flying tackle that separated me from Peggy and threw me back toward the open door. The sound of the gun exploded, deafening in the small space. Ben jerked backwards and collapsed on top of me. I knew, without doubt, that he meant to shield me.

"Go," he said, a look of terrible pain written on his face.

I remember the numbing sense of horror that he would die, even as I called his name and tried to stop the bleeding with my hands. There was blood everywhere, across his chest, his back, his neck, with no way to tell where it was all coming from—enough blood to make a red river across the hallway.

"Please, Daddy, please don't." Peggy was begging, holding on to her father's arm.

For one awful moment, I thought he was going to shoot her in the face from point-blank range and all but closed my eyes at the horror of it. His intentions were written clearly, spiritually, in every line of his countenance, like the hand of Abraham slaughtering a lamb.

Peggy knew it, too.

Her face crumpled in fear. She was on her knees, pitifully pleading, still desperate for affirmation of his love. One final time, she said, "Daddy…"

He blinked and everything changed. I didn't see it coming. Never expected it.

The gun wavered and steadied, the muscles tensing along his forearm. He reached his fingers out, almost touching her head. With the other hand, he put the gun against his right temple, and without hesitation, pulled the trigger.

Peggy's screams will haunt me the rest of my life.

Epilogue

Hollowell's bullet tore through Ben's back at an angle, cleaving muscle, bone, and tendon without discrimination, missing his heart by less than an inch. His luck was extraordinary.

Even then it was a close call for seventy-two hours.

It wasn't the first time he'd been wounded, but I wanted it to be the last. I didn't know if I could take the strain.

Peggy, who finally had to be sedated, will bear more scars than Ben, and no amount of loving arms will cure her soon. Her reaction brought back memories of the weeks after Daniel was murdered when I was unable to sleep or eat or stop crying.

Eloise, her mother's sister, took her back to Pennsylvania after three days. I liked her. She seemed just what Peggy needed for the long haul, and brought her to the hospital so Peggy could say goodbye and see for herself that Ben was alive.

In the dim waiting room, Peggy looked thinner, older. The baby roundness of her face had all but vanished, her eyes no longer those of a teenager.

"He loved my mother," she said. "I know he did. He told me it was an accident that she fell down the stairs. At first I believed him, but her suitcases were hidden under his bed with everything folded her own special way. All her jewelry was there, her makeup, even her Bible. That's what made me sure she'd planned to leave, why I knew he must have done something, somehow, to cause her fall. He left them under the bed as punishment, I think. The guilt just ate him up."

A leaden inertia had settled across my soul days before. I didn't know what to say to her.

As they were leaving, Peggy got as far as the nurse's station before turning back to give me one last hug. She said, "If it hadn't been for you, I'd be dead."

I watched her walk away and thought it a miracle that, after everything that had happened, she considered it a good thing to be alive. Davis, without whose intervention I would never have gotten involved in the first place, deserved the most gratitude. He, at least, hadn't damaged anyone in the process. I can't stop reflecting that if we had paid attention when she kept saying, "You don't understand," Kevin might still be alive.

So, like Peggy, I haven't been sleeping much, and remind myself often that when luck was being passed around in Hollowell's house, I received far more than my fair share.

Meanwhile, I walk the hospital hallways. Or visit Jinks. Or sit in Ben's room and wait for him to recognize me, to know I'm still living.

I talked with Sam the other day. He's selling the

Westchester property and says that everything has changed, that the business is in new hands. I don't know what that means. I don't want to.

Johnny smiled when I asked if they were short of money, but that was before I learned they were looking at oceanfront property on Wrightsville Beach. I'm glad, I think.

We don't yet know where Arthur is and I don't care, not after Johnny told me he had long suspected his hand in Daniel's death. He also says the word on the street is that Arthur is hiding out in Miami, which wouldn't surprise any of us, but it's only a rumor. There have been no more incidents.

Stan stopped by the hospital again this morning. He feels guilty that he didn't suspect Hollowell, and that no one in the department put two and two together when they learned that his wife had once been an accountant for Bill Burris Development.

In Hollowell's garage, Stan found a dark green Toyota with buckshot right where Randolph said it would be, along with Jinks's cell phone and empty aerosol paint cans in the trunk.

"I got the fingerprints I wanted," he said. "The bloody shoe was in his upstairs closet. From the bedroom window, he would have had a clear view of the path to the teahouse. I'm betting he had watched Burris use it before and was just waiting for the right time. Easy enough to spot his car in the parking lot. I suspect Hollowell was still at the scene that night when Peggy and Kevin came along."

"She told me she heard something *like a deer or a big dog*, and that Kevin said it was stupid. Even in the dark, Hollowell would know his own daughter's voice. From there, it wouldn't have taken much effort to find out who Kevin was."

"One of his neighbors saw him that night. She'd been out of town for four days when my men were going door to door and finally called us back."

"Mrs. Hanford with the crying baby. You can see quite a lot of things sitting in the dark at night, with or without a colicky child."

"She said Hollowell often went into the Arboretum with a flashlight to smoke cigars, just like Monday night, when she saw him come out his back door and cross the yard."

"If he thought his wife had the affair, it must have driven him half mad to watch Burris strut around the Arboretum. I wonder if that's why he went onto the grounds at night—waiting and hoping Burris would turn up?"

Stan held my hand for a moment. "There's something else we would have found out if we'd checked sooner. Hollowell had a medical discharge from the Army in the early nineties and was hospitalized last spring for depression."

"If you could have seen him…" I shook my head. "I can't feel sympathy for him yet, but I understand better what he was going through. At our first meeting,

Peggy told me he was still writing letters to his dead wife."

"We found them."

"Another one who couldn't sleep at night," I said.

He studied my face. "With good reason, apparently. The suitcases, the wife's picture still by his bedside… Go figure."

"Do you think he did the shooting at Sam's farm? I've wondered about that."

"We won't ever know for sure. Maybe Arthur was behind it. I don't think you have to worry about it, either way."

I nodded.

"You need anything, honey?" he said, getting to his feet.

"Just one thing."

Stan put his big arm around my shoulders. "I'd help if I could. We all would. You know that don't you?"

He's being careful around me, and Gran, Lucille, even Payton Gray are being nice, as if they imagine I'll fall apart like Peggy.

I won't.

The doctors are cutting back on Ben's pain medication, and earlier today he recognized me for the first time. I was sitting by his bedside, holding his hand, when he squeezed my fingers. His eyes were open and clear, focused for the first time in days.

"Hey," he whispered.

I wanted to say something witty, like *I have the*

worst luck with men. There was a lot I planned to say, but the truth is, he caught me by surprise, and the words got stuck in my throat.

I put his open palm against the side of my face and simply wept.

About the Author

Wanda Canada has been a writer, real estate broker, old house renovator, lobbyist, political candidate, full-time volunteer, and mother of three. Her first book, *Island Murders,* began the Carroll Davenport mystery series. She lives with her husband, John, on the Intracoastal Waterway near Wilmington, NC.